NOTHING
BUT
TROUBLE

ALSO BY JACQUELINE DAVIES

The Lemonade War
The Lemonade Crime
The Bell Bandit
The Candy Smash
The Magic Trap

Where the Ground Meets the Sky
Lost

The Boy Who Drew Birds
The Night Is Singing
The House Takes a Vacation
Tricking the Tallyman
Panda Pants

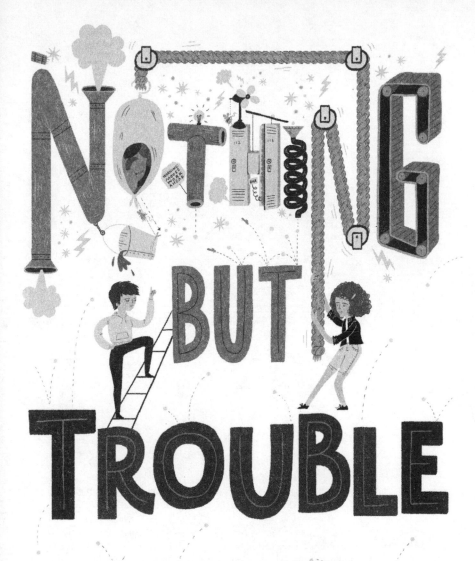

NOThING BUT TROUBLE

JACQUELINE DAVIES

KATHERINE TEGEN BOOKS
An Imprint of HarperCollins Publishers

Katherine Tegen Books is an imprint of HarperCollins Publishers.

Nothing But Trouble
Copyright © 2016 by Jacqueline Davies and HarperCollins Publishers
All rights reserved. Printed in the United States of America. No part of this book may be used or reproduced in any manner whatsoever without written permission except in the case of brief quotations embodied in critical articles and reviews. For information address HarperCollins Children's Books, a division of HarperCollins Publishers, 195 Broadway, New York, NY 10007.
www.harpercollinschildrens.com
ISBN 978-0-06-236988-8
Typography by Ellice M. Lee
16 17 18 19 20 CG/RRDH 10 9 8 7 6 5 4 3 2 1

First Edition

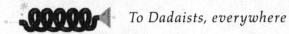 *To Dadaists, everywhere*

ONE

EXPLOSIONS ARE A FACT OF LIFE. At least they were in Maggie Gallagher's life. Her only goal was to keep them *quiet*—contained and undetected.

This morning, that hadn't worked out so well, despite the fact that she was down in the basement.

"What on God's green earth was that?" bellowed Grandpop from the first floor.

"Nothing, Grandpop!" shouted Maggie, waving her hands back and forth to clear the smoke. Although Maggie loved explosions, this one had been discouraging. Her summer-long quest to concoct the perfect fuel for a hydraulic press would have to wait. It was the first day of sixth grade and she was *late*.

Switching gears, she turned her attention to what she needed to get out the door, ticking off items on her mental list as she climbed each stair: Lunch money? *Check.* Backpack? *Check.* Combination lock for school locker? *Check.* Secret package on the front porch? *Check.* Hair clip? Hair clip—? Maggie frantically ran her fingers through her long, unruly hair. Oh, fizz! Her curly, out-of-control hair would just have to stay that way for the first day of school. Emily and Allie would scold her, but Maggie didn't care if her head looked like an explosion in progress.

How did it get to be so late?

Her grandfather followed her into the cramped kitchen, wheeling his chair over the worn bump of the threshold with a grunt of effort. "Sounded like you drove a pickup truck through a brick wall down there!" he said.

"No, just dropped something," said Maggie, wincing slightly at the lie. It was awful to admit, but ever since Grandpop had been confined to a wheelchair, it had been a whole lot easier to get away with things. For example, at this very moment, she had the entire vacuum cleaner laid out in pieces on the floor of her bedroom upstairs.

"Well, I hope you weren't messing with my stuff!" said Grandpop irritably. Maggie pictured the towering pile of auto parts he had collected over the years that became older and rustier the longer it was heaped in the basement. Then she reminded herself that she was doing *her* part to clean up that mess. She was *recycling*, after all. Still, she couldn't help feeling a snip of guilt as she thought of the secret package hidden on the porch.

"Grandpop, is there anything I can do for you before I go to school?" asked Maggie.

"'Bout time you asked!" Grandpop got crankier in the hot weather, which was saying something, because he was pretty grouchy in the winter, too. "Wheel me out to the porch where I can catch a breeze," he grumbled.

Maggie froze, her backpack hoisted on one shoulder. If she wheeled Grandpop out on the porch now, he would see her pick up the hidden box ready for mailing, and she couldn't risk him asking questions. Not about that!

"I'm so late, Grandpop!"

"Oh, for Pete's sake!" he said in complete exasperation. "Could you at least hand me a Moxie from the fridge before you run off?"

Maggie hurried to the refrigerator to grab the cold bottle of soda. Before he lost his leg, Maggie's grandfather had worked on the line for forty years at the Odawahaka Bottling Company, which bottled the sweet, fizzy soft drink that was the town's last remaining pride and joy. Maggie popped the top and handed the bottle to her grandfather, warning him, "That drink is nothing but high-fructose corn syrup, artificial coloring, and sodium benzoate."

"Ha! Shows what you know, Miss Smarty-Pants. It's got gentian root, and that's medicine. Good for digestion! Plus, it's only got two hundred and fifty calories per bottle."

"But you drink ten bottles a day!"

Her grandfather reached over to smack her one, but Maggie scooted past, shouting "Love you!" as she hightailed it out the door. On the front porch, she retrieved the large package hidden under a plastic tablecloth and began to head down the hill to Oda M. She needed to be quick if she was going to make it to the post office and still get to school before the first bell, but the package was heavy and kept slipping out of her grasp. And no matter what, she couldn't risk running into . . .

Oh no! There they were. Emily and Allie. And waiting for her, too. Maggie leaped behind the hedge that surrounded Mrs. Plainfield's house on the corner. She pushed the heavy package among the roots and wedged herself into the bush so that she could survey the scene without being spotted herself. Emily and Allie were her two best friends, but she couldn't tell them what was in the box. That was "top secret," which was one level higher than "best-friend secret." And anyway, lately

Maggie had been questioning if Allie and Emily really fit the category of "best friend" at all.

She wasn't able to hear what the girls were saying to each other, but there was a lot of chatter and laughter—the high-energy, slightly nervous kind you hear on the first day of school. And then the two spontaneously burst into song—probably one that they'd learned together at chorus camp over the summer. They were singing in harmony, Allie taking the high notes and Emily carrying the low. They sounded so perfect together, it made Maggie want to jump out of the bushes and say, "Here I am!" interrupting the song she couldn't sing and closing up the distance she'd been feeling ever since her friends had returned from camp. But then Allie messed up, and both girls collapsed in giggles, and something about the way they were laughing—*Was it possible to laugh in harmony?*—made Maggie squeeze farther into the bush.

Once they had stopped, Emily looked up the hill, past the bush that Maggie was hiding in, and said, "I don't think she's coming." Maggie could hear the disappointment in her voice.

"Maybe we missed her," said Allie. "At least we all have homeroom together."

"With Mrs. Matlaw!" sang Emily. And both girls started to run down the hill, singing yet another song that Maggie didn't know.

Maggie sighed. This was not the way you were supposed to feel about your two best friends.

"Do you hide in bushes a lot?"

Maggie stumbled backward out of the hedge, tripping over the package at her feet and falling to the ground.

A tall girl was standing on Mrs. Plainfield's lawn, and she laughed in a friendly way, reaching down to give Maggie a hand up.

"I never hide in bushes!" said Maggie, which was so completely untrue that even *she* started to laugh. The girl's grip was strong, and Maggie was back on her feet in an instant.

Maggie inspected the girl, who looked like she was in eighth or ninth grade. She had dark brown hair cut short in a stylish pixie with long, dramatic bangs that fell like a waterfall to one side. She was much taller than Maggie—but then again, just about everybody was—and she had a whole row of tiny, bright gemstone stud earrings circling the outside of one ear, which made Maggie think of a rainbow. The girl wore a white T-shirt with gray lettering across the front, but Maggie couldn't read the words because the leather strap of the girl's low-slung mailbag covered them up. No backpack for this girl. She was clearly from another planet.

Normally, Maggie would have asked a dozen questions—*What's your name? Where do you live? Did you get your ears pierced all at once or one at a time? What does your T-shirt say? Where do you come from? And why are you here?* It had been so long since Maggie had seen a strange face in Odawahaka that her natural curiosity went into overdrive. But for the moment, she just stared blankly, trying to organize her chaotic questions into some kind of reasonable marching order. The girl smiled pleasantly through the long pause, then pointed to Maggie's feet and asked, "What's in the box?"

The box!

Don't answer that! warned her father's voice inside her head.

Like a flock of birds that had been startled by a coyote's call, all of Maggie's questions took flight and scattered at once. She reached down and grabbed the box, apologizing as she backed away: "I'm so late! Sorry! The bus to the high school picks up in front of the Opera House." At least she could offer that piece of friendly welcome-to-town advice. Then she turned tail and hurried as fast as she could with the unwieldy package in her arms for the remaining two blocks to the post office. Thank goodness Emily and Allie were nowhere in sight.

TWO

"OOH, THAT'S A HEAVY ONE, HON!" said Mrs. Barrett, swiveling in her tall seat to stare over the post office counter. Behind her, she had hung a Wildcats banner to remind everyone about Friday's opening game—as if they needed reminding!

"I know!" said Maggie, heaving the package onto the postal scale. "I carried it."

And practically dropped it, reminded her father, unhelpfully.

"*Hush*," whispered Maggie, annoyed.

"What, sweetie?" asked Mrs. Barrett.

"Nothing!" She scooped up the unruly mess of curly blond hair that exploded from her head and whipped it into a messy knot. Without a hair clip, the whole thing would come undone within a minute. Oh well.

"Your mom's not taking you to school today?" Mrs. Barrett glanced toward the post office window as if she expected to see Maggie's mother, standing alone out there, peering in. The implied criticism of her mother managed to both annoy and sting Maggie at the same time.

"No," she said quickly. She was already reaching into her pocket for the money, wishing she could steer the conversation away from her mother. *Away, away, away.*

"I haven't seen her in *ages*. Now, when *I* went to Oda M," said Mrs. Barrett, slowly tapping away on her computer keyboard, "I always—"

"Mrs. Barrett!" said Maggie, trying not to let total panic overtake her as she looked at the cold face of the clock on the wall. "I'm super late! Can I just leave money and the package and then we'll figure it all out later?"

The smile disappeared from Mrs. Barrett's face. "No, dear. Perhaps if your mother had gotten you up earlier this morning, you wouldn't be in such a hurry now." She turned her attention back to her keyboard, murmuring, "I still can't believe they're tearing the old school down."

It was true that the Odawahaka Middle School was scheduled to be demolished. As the population of the town dwindled, the decrepit building had become too expensive to keep up. But neither the newer elementary school nor the high school could absorb Oda M's students all at once, so the plan was to peel each grade off, one year at a time. The eighth graders had been the first to go, followed by the fifth graders, and then the seventh graders. This year, only the sixth graders would be left to rattle through the halls of the mouse-infested school. A wrecking ball would reduce it to rubble once they moved on.

Mrs. Barrett continued to cluck as Maggie stifled an audible groan. "All the way to Texas!" said the postal clerk, punching the zip code into her keyboard. "My, my. That family of yours." And there was more than a hint of disapproval in her voice. "You do send packages all over, don't you?"

This kind of "neighborly interest" was just one of the many terrible things about living in a town as small as Odawahaka, and just one of the many, many reasons Maggie couldn't wait to get *out*.

Mrs. Barrett stared at her. "Thirty-one dollars and fifty-three cents. It'll get there by Friday."

Maggie pushed thirty-two dollars across the counter and said, "Keep the change! I'm late!" Then she ran for the door. Odawahaka Middle School was just eight blocks away and all downhill, but the first bell would ring any minute, and Maggie would have to run the whole way. Her careful plan had been to get to school *early*, and now she would hardly make it there before the beginning of homeroom.

"I can't keep the change!" called Mrs. Barrett after her. "It messes up my cashing out!" But Maggie was gone and flying down the hill, her wild hair bursting out of its makeshift bun and streaming like tightly curled yellow party ribbons behind her. Flying past Quinn, past Main, past Kline and South, all the streets she had known her entire life. Flying into her future, but also to the school that held the memories of her family's past and everything that had gone wrong.

Maggie couldn't wait for it to be demolished.

THREE

THE FIRST BELL WAS JUST RINGING as Maggie bounded through
the front doors and stood in the entryway of Odawahaka Middle School. It had been a grand building when
it was first constructed nearly eighty years ago. There
was a small rotunda overhead, and in the center of the
tiled floor, right in front of the main office, was a large
bronze statue of the town mascot: a lunging wildcat with
its fangs bared and claws extended. It was kind of scary,
but to the citizens of Odawahaka, the statue meant just
one thing: this was *Wildcat Country*, and the town took
great pride in its high school football team.

These days, it seemed like the only thing the town
still had to be proud of.

Maggie's heart was beating fast from running, but
she needn't have worried about receiving a tardy slip.

Pandemonium had overtaken the entire building.

The lockers, defenseless without any combination locks, were under attack. Students were flipping open the doors and then moving on instantly to the next as if in search of hidden treasure. Other students were simply banging the doors shut for the pleasure of the noise that rebounded and echoed in the high-ceilinged hallway. And still other students were racing toy cars up and down the hall or throwing tennis balls so that they ricocheted off the walls, lockers, and the Wildcat statue. The noise put Maggie's morning explosion to shame.

All of a sudden, a zooming toy car hit Maggie's sneaker and flipped over on itself. She reached down to pick it up. There was a small rubber mouse jammed into the driver's seat, as if the mouse had taken control of the machine.

Max Pruitt ran up to her to retrieve the car. In his hand, he held a rip cord. "Listen to this," he shouted to Maggie over the incredible noise in the hallway. He loaded the rip cord into the car and pulled with all his might. The car let out a mighty *ROAR!* When he placed it on the floor, the car and mouse took off at an incredible speed. Maggie quickly estimated that if you took into account the size of the car, it was traveling at the equivalent of four hundred miles per hour. *Wow*, she thought. *I didn't think those things could go that fast.*

Dozens of toy cars raced up and down the hall, and hundreds of tennis balls rolled about madly, like gerbils set free from their cages. One tennis ball sailed through the air and whacked Maggie on the shoulder. She picked it up and smiled when she saw that the word *ROAR* was written on it with Sharpie pen in careful block letters.

She bounced the tennis ball so high it flew over her head and hit the ceiling, then began an interesting pattern of diminishing oscillation that she would have liked to study, but Grace McHenry grabbed the ball and was off with it.

"Maggie!" squealed Emily as she and Allie ran up to her. "We waited on the corner but figured you'd gone ahead. And then we saw this!"

"What's happening?" asked Maggie. "Why is everyone going nuts?"

"Lyle was the first one to discover it!" said Allie as all three girls linked arms and walked toward homeroom, dodging balls and race cars as they went. "We were all just standing around in the hallway, waiting for the homeroom teachers to let us in, and Lyle started opening lockers just because . . . well, who ever knows why Lyle does what he does?"

"He was probably looking for food," said Emily.

"He's always looking for food," said Maggie. All three girls had known Lyle Whittaker since kindergarten, when he famously ate twelve rubber bands during one recess period.

"So he just happened to flip open this one locker," said Allie, "and about a hundred tennis balls came spilling out! All over the floor! So then other kids started opening lockers and found the cars. And that was all it took. The whole place has gone completely insane!"

"Who's that?" asked Maggie, spotting a man in a suit and tie who didn't look much older than Emily's college-age brother. He had commandeered one of the toy race cars and was playing with the rip cord, running it back and forth to create an impressive roaring noise, as if he was itching to let 'er rip.

"That's the new math teacher, Mr. Platt," said Allie. "He's cute, don't you think?" And she squeezed Maggie's arm as if they both felt exactly the same way about this.

Maggie made a face. Ever since getting back from chorus camp that summer, Emily and Allie had started talking about which boys were "cute" and which boys were "supercute." Maggie didn't get it. Boys were just . . . boys. The same as they'd always been. And math teachers? It was not possible for a math teacher to be cute.

As if to prove her point, Max and Tyler came bar-reling toward them. "Comin' through!" yelled Max as they crashed through the trio of girls, breaking them up, then set up their race cars at the far end of the hall in an attempt to set a distance record. Emily and Allie laughed, but Maggie was as interested as the boys to see how far the cars could go.

"Oh, girls!" said Mrs. Matlaw, coming toward Emily, Allie, and Maggie with a metal wastebasket extended. Mrs. Matlaw taught Language Arts, but there were times she seemed more like a mother than a teacher. "Could you help me? These tennis balls! Someone is going to fall, I just know it!" Maggie reached down to scoop up one of the fuzzy balls as it rolled by. Even though the girls had been fifth graders at Oda M last year, they knew all the sixth-grade teachers. It was a small town, and they were just as likely to bump into Mrs. Matlaw at Weis Market as the halls of Oda M. Maggie had known Mrs. Matlaw since kindergarten, and she was happy that she was going to have her for homeroom this year.

As Maggie deposited a tennis ball in the metal waste-basket, she caught sight of Kayla Gold, who was wearing an outfit that Maggie knew had been purchased in the fashionable stores in Wilkes-Barre, or maybe even as far away as Philadelphia. Kayla was smiling. That *smile*. Those *teeth*. Her perfect hair. Even from down the hall, Maggie couldn't help but notice that Kayla Gold *glowed*. And it was the puzzle of Maggie's life that she and Kayla had once been best friends.

FOUR

"LOOK!" SHOUTED ALLIE, POINTING DOWN THE hall to where the bronze Wildcat statue was mounted on its impressive stone pedestal. Something was hanging above the Wildcat's head that had not been there before.

"How did *that* happen?" asked Maggie. She was always more interested in the *how* of something than the *what*.

The sixth graders converged around the statue and looked up. Stretched across the opening of the rotunda was a square white sheet, pulled tight by invisible strings that attached it to the old stone walls of the building. Dangling below the sheet was a toy mouse in a small harness. The harness was attached by thin strings to the four corners of the white sheet.

"What does it say?" asked Brianna. The mouse was

holding a sign, but the letters were small and the mouse hung high above their heads.

Colt DuPrey, who spent so much of his time reading quietly to himself, deciphered the message first. "Pull my tail!"

Everyone laughed, but Max didn't wait to hear the order a second time. Unable to resist the call to misbehave, he scrambled onto the back of the Wildcat statue.

"Max!" shouted Mrs. Matlaw. "You'll fall and hurt yourself. Get down immediately!" Then she turned to Mr. Peebles, the elderly social studies teacher, and asked with more fury in her voice than Maggie had ever heard from her, "Where is our new principal! How is it possible to be late on the *first* day of school?"

Sadly for Max, he couldn't reach the dangling tip of the mouse's tail no matter how hard he tried. He withdrew in defeat. Classmates started to chant, "Lyle, Lyle, Lyle," because Lyle was by far the tallest boy in the class. Lyle, who had been leaning against a wall, contentedly sipping a can of Moxie—no doubt his breakfast—with his eyes half-closed, shrugged and stepped forward.

"Lyle!" called Mrs. Matlaw with concern.

"I'll be fine, Mrs. M," said Lyle casually. "Don't sweat it." Then he burped really loudly, climbed onto the back of the Wildcat statue, and yanked the mouse's tail.

The sheet snapped free from the walls of the rotunda, releasing dozens of helium-filled balloons. The students oohed and aahed at the sight. Even Mrs. Matlaw whispered, "How beautiful!" As the balloons took flight, the sheet became the mouse's parachute, and the mouse, still in its custom-made harness, floated down, landing on the back of the Wildcat statue.

Each balloon had a colorful ribbon attached to it with a small cellophane package tied to its end. As the weight of the packages pulled the balloons down toward the ground, the students' state of quiet awe turned to frenzy as they jumped to capture them, each eager to figure out what was tied to the end of the balloons. The hallway once again erupted in noise and chaos. Lyle was the first to unwrap the cellophane. "Cheese!" he announced with satisfaction, and popped the piece of cheddar into his mouth.

"Look what it says on the balloons," said Emily, catching one and showing it to Maggie and Allie. The balloon had the word *ROAR!* written on it in black ink.

There was bedlam in the hallway as helium balloons flew around the corridor, batted back and forth by the students. Some of the girls attached them to their bracelets (after handing the cheese to Lyle, who ate it all), and Tyler helped Max tie as many as possible to his shorts with the hope that he might achieve liftoff. The din in the hallway rose to *Guinness World Records* level.

Suddenly, there was the sound of wood smashing into metal. Maggie spun around. A man she'd never seen before was standing next to a dented-in locker with a baseball bat in his hand. He was stocky and strong, square-jawed with a buzz cut that made his head look like a block of wood. "Homerooms! NOW!" he shouted.

The students scattered. Even the teachers scurried out of the hall.

"New principal!" squeaked Emily as the three girls hurried to follow Mrs. Matlaw.

But when they approached the door, Mrs. Matlaw rested a hand on Maggie's shoulder and said sympathetically, "You've been reassigned, hon. Along with a few others from the other classes. You're going to be in homeroom . . . B-1."

"Oh!" said Emily softly, looking like she might begin to cry. She reached out to give Maggie's hand a squeeze, as if this might be the last time they ever saw each other alive. Allie gave Maggie a quick hug and the kind of smile that tried, but failed, to be encouraging; then both girls ducked into Mrs. Matlaw's room. Maggie was left speechless, standing in the hall, her friends gone.

Didn't see that coming, whispered her father in her ear.

It was one of his favorite expressions, scrawled throughout his notebooks whenever something unexpected happened, throwing off his calculations.

"You know the way," Mrs. Matlaw said to the confused group of students she had gathered. She looked genuinely concerned. "Be brave!" she called after them as they straggled away.

B-1, thought Maggie. *Oh no.*

FIVE

ABOUT A DOZEN STUDENTS MARCHED—as if to their deaths—down the dim, echoey stairs to the basement of Odawahaka Middle School, where the empty and abandoned science rooms remained—their doors closed, their lab tables covered in dust, visited only by the mice that occasionally ventured out of the walls. Physics. *Gone.* Biology. *Gone.* Engineering. *Gone.* Only one science teacher remained at the doomed school: Mrs. Dornbusch. But everyone knew that the oldest and most feared teacher in the history of Odawahaka didn't supervise homeroom. She had been freed from that burden years ago. So why were they being sent to her room?

Whatever the reason, the Dungeon Dragon was waiting for them, standing at the door to her secluded lair, one clawlike hand gripping the doorknob. At five feet eleven inches tall, she was a towering column of gray: straight, salt-and-pepper hair spilling over her forehead and spouting out around her ears; loose gray sweatpants that collected in a puddle around her ankles; and a gray Susquehanna University sweatshirt with the sleeves pushed up to her knobby elbows. Layered underneath the sweatshirt was a sky-blue turtleneck that highlighted the startling, watery blueness of her large, bulging eyes. Two small, gold hoop earrings curled around her massive earlobes. The earrings looked like mountain climbers desperately clinging to a dangerous ledge.

One by one, the students in her homeroom passed in front of her—Chris Shuman, Brianna Willits, Riley Hughes, Colt DuPrey, Jenna Mack, Becky Burroughs, Stevie Jencks, Grace McHenry, Shana Delaney, Lyle Whittaker, Max Pruitt, and Tyler Grady—and to each one, the Gray Gargoyle hissed, "You're late!"

Maggie was the last to approach the door. When she did, Mrs. Dornbusch stuck out a bony arm, barring her way. "You're that *girl*," she said, narrowing her eyes in disapproval.

Maggie tensed slightly. She had a reputation, just as her mother had had when she was growing up in Odawahaka. The Smart Girl. Last year's teachers always informed next year's teachers: *Expect great work from*

Maggie Gallagher. Maggie didn't like the spotlight. She would have preferred to stay hidden. You could get more done that way.

"Starts with an *M*," continued Mrs. Dornbusch, holding up her hand to silence Maggie. "Not Mary. Not Molly. Not Martha." She shook her head. "Doesn't matter. Inside."

"That's where I was going," said Maggie.

"Your *mother* . . . ," said the Dungeon Dragon, unexpectedly barring the door again. Maggie froze. She stared at the formidable woman, a colossal fountain of gray with eyes that pierced like two needle-sharp icicles. "I remember your mother. She was a suck-up."

Maggie stiffened but didn't look away. She stared back into those pools of ice-cold blue.

That's my girl, whispered her father.

"But she *left*," said the teacher, drumming against the door frame. "She got a full scholarship to a big-name school. Are you telling me she came *back*?"

"Yes," said Maggie.

"What a waste," murmured Mrs. Dornbusch. She pointed to the classroom. "Go!"

Maggie went inside and chose a seat near the back. With so few students in the classroom, it was going to be hard to hide.

The B-1 Bomber approached the ancient blackboard, chose a large piece of chalk from its silver tray, and wrote in giant letters: *I.D.C.*

"Listen up!" she said, settling onto the edge of her desk, her long legs stretched in front of her, her arms folded across her chest. "I have been teaching at Odawahaka Middle School for *thirty-eight* years. I've taught your brothers, your sisters, your parents, and, in one or two cases, your *grand*parents. And in recognition for my years of service, our former principal, Mr. Watts, relieved me of the duty of supervising homeroom." She glared at every last student in the room, one at a time.

"Well! After two thousand, four hundred and forty-six students, I am finally retiring. And make no mistake, I am *counting the days*." She pointed without looking to a corner of the blackboard that bore the number *180* outlined severely in chalk. "But our new principal, Mr. Shute, has decided in his *infinite wisdom* that I should once again supervise homeroom."

Someone coughed. Maggie wasn't sure, but she thought it was Riley Hughes, who had a lot of allergies and pretty bad asthma that flared up in stressful situations. Mold, chalk dust, and conflict were a potent combo for Riley's highly reactive airways.

"And so my motto for this, my *final* year," said Mrs.

Dornbusch, "can be summed up in three words." She returned to the blackboard and retraced each letter as she announced, "I. Don't. Care.

"You have a problem at home? I don't care. Your dog died? I don't care. You're hemorrhaging from an open wound? I don't care.

"Let me be clear: I am not here to babysit, coddle, foster self-esteem, collect permission slips, deal with your dysfunctional families, build community, or lead everyone in a sing-along. I am a science teacher. So don't—let me repeat—*don't* come to me with your joys or sorrows. Why? Because: I. Don't. Care." For emphasis, she pounded the blackboard with each word she uttered, until the chalk splintered and sent shards flying into the front row of students. Lyle picked up a piece, popped it into his mouth, and started to chew on it thoughtfully.

Just then Kayla Gold sailed in.

Perfect timing, Maggie thought. *As usual.*

"I'm so sorry we're late," Kayla said, smiling broadly at Mrs. Dornbusch.

We? Had Kayla finally gone to the limit and adopted the royal "we" in describing herself? She was the class president, at least until the next election was held. But even for someone as aspirational and supremely confident as Kayla, it seemed a bit much to call herself "we."

But then a girl followed Kayla into the room—the same girl Maggie had met on her way to school. Pixie cut. Rainbow stud earrings. Warm smile.

The new girl.

Maggie could see that Kayla was pleased with her trophy. "Principal Shute asked me to be the ambassador for our new student," she continued, all eyes on her. "Here are our tardy slips." She smiled again and handed Mrs. Dornbusch two official blue passes, which were hoarded by the school secretary, Mrs. McDermott, as if they were ingots of gold.

Mrs. Dornbusch threw the passes in the trash can. She glared at Kayla, perhaps with the intention of shrinking her down to size with her vinegary stare, like pouring salt on a slug. But Kayla, as Maggie had once realized, was like a self-contained vector force field: $\vec{F}(\vec{k})$, where $\vec{F}$ is the overpowering force exerted on anyone who comes in contact with Kayla $(\vec{k})$. In other words: once you came into her range, it was hard not to get sucked into the vortex.

"Everyone," Kayla said, addressing the class, "this is Lena Polachev. She just moved to town. Let's give her a Wildcat Welcome!"

As if on cue, the entire class began the chant, "Huh, huh, huh, huh, ME-OW," slashing the air with their

"Wildcat" claws on the final syllable. Everyone joined in.

Except for Maggie.

It wasn't that she was against the chant itself, or even the football team it supported. And it wasn't that she didn't want to make the new girl feel welcome. She just hated anything that required her to follow the herd. Group costumes, group singing, group work, and most of all, group cheering.

And the Odawahaka Wildcats cheer was the groupiest of all group activities. At every football game, the whole school recited the cheer en masse. Maggie had her own football cheers, her favorite being: "Momentum equals mass times velocity! Go, Wildcats!" Not surprisingly, she couldn't get even Emily and Allie to join her on that one.

When the whole class "meowed," Lena laughed and then sat down in the empty chair right in front of Maggie. She turned and looked at her, as if to say, *Hey, I remember you.*

"Are you finished?" Mrs. Dornbusch asked drily, looking at Kayla, who was still standing at the front of the class. "Or would you like to lead us in another form of synchronized lunacy?"

"No, ma'am," said Kayla, casting her eye about for an empty seat near Lena. "Jenna," she said calmly. "Would you mind sitting in a different seat so I can sit next to Lena? I'm her school ambassador."

Without a blink, Jenna gathered up her things and moved. *Force field in action*, thought Maggie. Kayla smiled and said, "Just doing my duty!" She settled into the chair as though it had been saved for her and smoothed her long, honey-colored hair so that it fell in perfect waterfalls around her blemish-free face. Maggie had to admit, the girl had swag.

The B-1 Bomber didn't agree. "Suck-up," she muttered, turning back to the blackboard and replacing the shattered piece of chalk in the metal tray.

"Mrs. Dornbusch," Lyle asked, raising his hand. "When you say you *don't care*, do you mean we don't have to show up to homeroom at all?"

Mrs. Dornbusch stared out the window, across the creek to the beautiful hills that rimmed the southern edge of town, and murmured, "If only." Then she snapped her head around and caught them in her frozen glare. "But, no. You have to show up, and so do I. But while you are here, you will get nothing from me, and I will ask nothing of you. Talk on your phones, copy your classmate's homework, play endless rounds of paper football, make each other cry—I. Don't. Care."

Lyle raised his hand again. "Can we use the Bunsen

burners to set fire to things?" he asked. "Not big things. Just little things? Carefully?"

The Dungeon Dragon looked at him through narrowed eyes, and her nostrils flared visibly. *Who needs a Bunsen burner?* Maggie thought, imagining fire streaming out of Mrs. Dornbusch's nose, leaving nothing behind but a sad pile of Lyle ashes.

Before the B-1 Bomber could answer, the new principal strode into the room through the open door, still carrying his baseball bat.

"Good morning, students," he said. "Mrs. Dornbusch." He nodded once in her direction, making it clear that there was no love lost between them. "I am Principal Shute." Mrs. Dornbusch glared at him. To Maggie it looked like she was sizing him up: already imagining him stuffed and mounted, determining if he might make a worthy trophy in her game room.

Principal Shute stood with his two feet planted hip-width apart, both hands resting on the top of the baseball bat. Mrs. Dornbusch, meanwhile, continued to slouch, leaning on the edge of her desk. She was taller than Mr. Shute by several inches. Even reclining, she gave the impression of looking down on him. But Mr. Shute had the mass, thought Maggie, her eyes shifting back and forth between the two. Height may be an advantage in an old-fashioned battle, but increased mass would always win the day when acceleration came into play. *Force equals mass times acceleration.* Maggie pulled out a piece of paper to do the calculations.

"As you may have heard by now," continued the principal, "I was in the Marine Corps. In the corps, our motto is *Semper fidelis.* Mr. Esposito will tell you that's Latin for 'Always loyal.' And I expect loyalty in return." He paused long enough for that statement to sink in.

"Now," he continued, his voice growing decidedly less welcoming. "We had an incident this morning, and property was damaged. I want to be clear: I will not have it. It is my mission to make sure this school operates in an orderly fashion. I take that mission very seriously, and so will you. Odawahaka Middle School is our *corps*, and I am your *captain*." He looked piercingly at the class.

Maggie could feel it. Groupiness. She was being corralled, herded, led by the nose. They all were. And she didn't like it. She raised her hand, and Mr. Shute nodded curtly in her direction, giving her permission to speak.

"What property damage was there?" she asked. "I mean, besides the locker you demolished?"

Principal Shute didn't move. "What is your name, young lady?"

"Maggie Gallagher."

An unpleasant smile spread across Mr. Shute's face. "I've heard about you."

Turning his attention back to the rest of the class, he announced severely, "Following this morning's incident, I've decided to institute a new school-wide policy: All students will eat lunch at *assigned* tables in the cafeteria. No changing seats. No leaving your table during lunchtime. No exceptions."

The class groaned just as the bell rang. "Dismissed!" he shouted, then walked out.

"One point five," whispered Maggie, stuffing her calculations into her notebook.

Force equals mass times acceleration. If Mrs. Dornbusch and Principal Shute were placed on a single track and approached each other at identical rates of acceleration in a head-on collision, Shute would create one and a half times the force of the B-1 Bomber, thus obliterating her. It was a formidable difference.

Maggie wondered how the rest of the year would go—if Day One started off with a bang like this.

SIX

AT LUNCH, MAGGIE WAS ASSIGNED TO Table 10, along with half her homeroom: Lyle, Max, Tyler, Jenna, Colt, Kayla—and the new girl.

Emily and Allie were assigned to Table 1, which wasn't even close enough to pass notes. In fifth grade, the girls had eaten lunch together every day. This year, clearly, would be different. But Maggie had known things would be different even before Mr. Shute assigned tables. For four weeks that summer, Emily and Allie had attended a church-sponsored sleep-away chorus camp on the shores of Lake Melody in Lackawanna State Forest. They had spent their days practicing harmonies and breathing techniques, learning about things that Maggie had never even heard of: vocal breaks and counterpoints, respiration and phonation. Then again, Maggie couldn't even carry a tune.

But as she set her cardboard tray on the table, she was shocked to recognize a feeling she hadn't expected: *relief.* She felt relieved not to be sitting at the same table with Allie and Emily, the silent bump on the log as they burst forth into glorious song.

Maggie sat down at the round cafeteria table with its eight attached stools. The tables were bright green and always made Maggie think of an octopus offering a pie at the end of each of its eight tentacles. Two seats over sat Colt DuPrey—by Maggie's estimation the quietest kid in the class. In fact, by the time Maggie sat down at the table, he had already settled into a book, reading as he ate his baloney sandwich. Lena promptly sat down in the empty seat between Maggie and Colt.

"Those are kind of . . . harsh," said Lena, and Maggie saw that she was looking at the two dusty, old football banners that hung on either side of the cafeteria clock. Behind the banners was a kind of balcony. From there you could look down on the entire cafeteria.

"The banners?" Maggie examined them. One read, *There is no substitute for STRENGTH and no excuse for a LACK OF IT.* The other one read, *The PRIDE and*

STRENGTH *of the Odawahaka Wildcats will not be entrusted to the TIMID or the WEAK*. Both displayed the image of the fierce, lunging Wildcat.

"Are they supposed to be . . . inspiring? Or powerful?" asked Lena.

Maggie shrugged. "I don't even notice them anymore. They've been there forever."

Kayla arrived and asked Colt, "Could you slide down, please? I'm supposed to sit next to Lena," with that peculiar mix of politeness and impatience that only Kayla could get away with. Without a word, Colt marked his place in his book and moved down to make room for Kayla.

How does she do it? Maggie wondered.

"Now that's power," whispered Lena to Maggie, as if she were reading her thoughts. Maggie and Lena laughed, which brought a scowl to Kayla's face as she opened her carton of milk.

The one and only topic of conversation at Table 10 that day was the morning's crazy prank. Max and Tyler were convinced that it was the work of some seventh-grade students who were mocking the sixth graders for being left behind in the falling-down old school when every other class had moved on. "We're the class that no one wants," Max explained to Lena, spinning on his stool as he ate his french fries.

"That is not true!" argued Kayla. "We are *not* the class that no one wants!"

"Yes, we are," insisted Max. "The school's going to be torn down, and we're the class that has to spend another year in this crypt. It'll probably fall down while we're still here and then we'll be"—he made his voice ghosty—"*buried alive!*"

"Stop it!" ordered Kayla. She turned to Lena. "They just need to make space for us. That's all. And there just wasn't . . ." Kayla looked for a prettier way to say it, but then gave up. "There just wasn't enough money."

"The town is broke," crowed Max, continuing to spin on his pie-shaped stool.

"Quit it," said Kayla impatiently. "Back to this morning—*I* think it might have been the teachers who did everything, as a special welcome back, since we're the very last class at Oda M."

"Yeah, maybe it was that psycho math teacher, Mr. Platt," said Tyler. "He's not normal! Did you notice all the cat stuff in his room?"

Everyone had. In addition to a cat poster that announced *New! Robotics Club! Meetings on Tuesdays after school!*, Mr. Platt had a cat stapler, a cat bobblehead, cat bookends, and a digital cat stopwatch that meowed to signal the end of timed quizzes. He even had a giant stuffed toy lion lounging on top of his filing cabinet.

"So he likes cats!" said Maggie. "That doesn't mean he filled our lockers with tennis balls." Maggie didn't like sloppy logic.

But Lyle had an entirely original theory: he insisted that the prank was the work of the fabled mice of Oda M. After all, it had been well known for years that burrows of mice lived in the walls of the old building. They could be heard scurrying about when students were taking tests or when anyone entered the building after dark. And there were all kinds of stories of "mouse mischief" that had taken place over the years. Lyle held up a ketchup-covered finger and pronounced in a somber voice, "It has been foretold: the mice are finally coming out of the walls." Then he licked the ketchup off his finger, causing a chorus of groans to rise from Table 10.

Mr. Esposito wandered by, smiling blandly. "Slow down, Maximus," he said gently, resting his hands on Max's shoulders to bring his spinning to a stop. Mr. Esposito taught French and Spanish to the students at Oda M, but his real passion was Latin. It was his dream to someday teach the language of Cicero and Ovid to the students in Odawahaka. So far, no one seemed the least bit interested. "A *modicum* of *decorum*. For as the great poet Virgil said, '*Durate et vosmet rebus servate secundis.*' Yes. Yes, indeed!" He wandered off, his eyes slightly misty behind his thick glasses.

The students at Table 10 held back their laughter until Mr. Esposito was out of earshot.

"He's another nut!" said Max. And the arguing continued about who had been responsible for turning a boring first day of school into a morning the students would never forget.

"Oh, gross!" said Kayla, pulling a long piece of blond hair from her lunch tray. "This is one of yours!" she yelled at Maggie.

Maggie shrugged. "Extra protein. It's good for you."

Kayla balled the offensive strand of hair into a napkin and threw it at Maggie. "Your hair is a menace to society," she said. "Why don't you *do* something with it? Instead of just letting it grow like it's some kind of wild plant!"

Before Maggie could respond that she actually *liked* her hair just the way it was, Lena turned to face her and Maggie was finally able to read the lettering on her T-shirt. It said: *Dada Is My Daddy.* When Maggie saw it, she laughed so suddenly that she inhaled a piece of hamburger. She reached for her carton of milk and tried to guzzle it to wash the burger chunk down, but because she was still laughing so hard, the milk sprayed out of her nose. That got Max and Tyler going, and pretty soon everyone at Table 10 was in hysterics. Everyone except Kayla. "That is dis*gust*ing!" she declared.

It was true: bits of hamburger were scattered across the table, doused in puddles of milk—which had *traveled through Maggie's nose*. It *was* disgusting. But Maggie didn't care. She hadn't laughed that hard in a long time. She certainly didn't laugh like that with Emily and Allie.

Maggie gathered up most of the hamburger bits and placed them on a napkin. (Lyle was eyeing the napkin, but even he wouldn't eat nose-milk-doused hamburger . . . would he?) Pointing at Lena's T-shirt, Max asked, "So what's Dada?"

Maggie jumped in and said, "It was this weird, *weird* art movement that happened after World War I, when all the artists were fed up with how horrible things were and how ugly the war had been, and they made art that basically said, 'The world doesn't make any sense and neither do we.' And they called it Dada, because Dada doesn't mean anything."

Lena nodded. "And when she says weird, she means *weird*. Like they painted a beard and a mustache on a picture of the Mona Lisa and said, 'It's art!' Or they put a urinal on a pedestal and said, 'It's art!'"

Lyle's eyes opened wide for a moment. "Gross!" he said with enthusiasm, then returned to his habitual state of sleepiness.

"That's the dumbest name ever," said Max. "Dada? It sounds like a baby."

"That's kind of the point," said Maggie.

"But it *was* art," said Lena, "because it made people think and feel. And it was political, too. They wanted to protest the war, and they got people to look at the world in a different way. Which is pretty cool." She smiled at Maggie. "You still have . . ." She pointed to her upper lip, and Maggie swiped at some milk that clung to her face.

Maggie smiled back at Lena. She was feeling so good, she didn't even get that prickly feeling that usually came just before a Kayla attack.

"A urinal!" said Kayla, her wide smile flashing, her teeth sparkling like jewels in a necklace. "That reminds me of something that happened that was *so funny.* Do you remember, Maggie, the time you were over at my house and you peed all over the kitchen floor? We were playing—I don't even remember what it was we were doing—"

"It was Legos," said Maggie. "We were building a

castle together." She felt her chest tighten and her face flush.

Don't let her get to you, whispered her father in her ear.

Max and Tyler started to snicker. Of course, everyone at the table had heard this story before. It was a small town, and the humiliations of your childhood followed you forever. But there was one person at the table who hadn't heard this story—Lena—and Maggie knew that Kayla's performance was just for her. Jenna giggled nervously. Colt kept his head down, reading his latest adventure series book. And Lyle had torn off a chip of cardboard from his lunch tray and was eating it.

"Right. Legos!" squealed Kayla, turning to Lena. "It was amazing. She stood up and just a flood of pee started to pour out of her. I mean—a *river.* And she made this huge puddle on the floor and my mom had to clean it up, which she was really not happy about. I mean, can you blame her? Somebody else's pee!"

"Kayla! We were in first grade." They had each drunk about a gallon of lemonade, and Maggie was really concentrating on the castle . . . and then it happened. She knew explaining or defending herself was not going to help. Arguing just made the story stick in people's minds even more. But why did Kayla have to bring it up on the first day of school?

"Who pees their pants when they're six?" asked Kayla. "I can't *ever* remember having an accident."

"Oh, I peed in my pants a tiny bit just last week," said Lena, waving her hand casually. "What's the big deal?" She looked at the frozen faces around the table and smiled her warm, friendly smile. "Oh, come on! We've all done it! I say if you've never wet your pants from laughing hard, then you've never *really* laughed."

Lyle nodded his head soberly. "That is an undisputable truth."

And after a split second of stunned silence, everyone at the table started to laugh. Including Maggie.

Kayla, however, looked furious. She got up and walked away to dump her lunch tray in the trash barrel.

Serves her right, said her father. And Maggie couldn't help agreeing.

While the others went back to arguing about the identity of the prankster—and if he or she would strike again—Maggie watched as Lena took a sketchbook out of her shoulder bag and began to draw something with her pencil. Her hands moved quickly, and she seemed completely absorbed in her work.

As Maggie passed Lena on the way to the trash

barrel, she looked over Lena's shoulder and saw that she had drawn a mouse—one that looked so real, you would think you were staring at a photograph. Underneath the drawing, Lena had written:

```
R        O        A        R
O        R                 I
D        G                 O
E        A                 T
N        N
T        I
S        Z
         E
```

SEVEN

AFTER SCHOOL, ALLIE AND EMILY ASKED Maggie if she wanted to come with them to the high school. They were going to try out for the school chorus. There was no middle school chorus this year; instead, all clubs and teams had been consolidated at the high school. Allie's mother had promised to drive them to Bloomsburg for ice cream afterward.

"I'm kind of tired," said Maggie, which was true. She'd hardly gotten any sleep last night. Besides, sitting around while Emily and Allie practiced scales and vocalizations didn't sound like much fun.

Maggie started the uphill trek alone. A pickup truck passed her as she crossed Pine Street, and she noticed that it sported the town's favorite bumper sticker:

What This Country Needs Is Plenty of MOXIE!

Typical Odawahaka, thought Maggie. She couldn't help brooding as she walked, thinking about Allie and Emily auditioning together. The three had been a team for so long—ever since Kayla had dumped Maggie in the first grade—that it was hard to think of Emily and Allie doing something just the two of them. But Maggie couldn't quite hide from herself this inconvenient fact: she hadn't really missed them while they were at chorus camp.

Maggie had just crossed Main and was still second-guessing her decision not to go with Allie and Emily, when she heard someone calling her name. She turned to see Lena.

"Can I walk home with you?" Lena asked Maggie after crossing the street.

"Afraid of getting lost?" It was a small-town joke. Getting lost in Odawahaka would be like getting lost inside a cereal box.

Lena laughed. Maggie was beginning to see that Lena was a girl who laughed easily. She wondered if there was a trick to that, or if some people were just born that way. And others not.

"No," said Lena. "I just thought . . . tough day. First

46

day in a new school. You know?" Maggie was surprised. Lena had made it all seem so easy.

"Actually," said Maggie, "I can't even imagine what it's like to be the new kid in town." *Kind of nice, I bet.* "Come on. It's all uphill from here."

As they walked, Lena reached into her shoulder bag and took out a camera. "Can I take a picture of you?" she asked.

Maggie gave her a strange look. "Why?"

"I take pictures of everything. Absolutely everything." Lena fiddled with the lens ring, snapping a few test shots to check the aperture setting. Maggie didn't know much about cameras, but she could tell that this was an expensive piece of equipment. "You have no idea how hard it was to leave my camera in my bag all day at school. I am *never* without my camera. It's like a part of my body." She raised the camera to her eye. "So . . . can I take a picture?"

"I suppose . . . ," said Maggie, and Lena snapped four or five pictures in rapid succession, then circled around Maggie and snapped another half dozen.

"Stop it!" said Maggie, laughing self-consciously. "You said *one.* Why do you need so many?"

"Because I make art. And it takes a lot of material to make art." She swooped in and took a close-up of

Maggie's nose, then one of her left ear, then one of a single long curl of her out-of-control hair. "You have the most gorgeous hair I've ever seen on a human being! It's like"—she reached out and touched a soft tendril—"the kind of hair a fairy would have. The best kind of fairy!" Then she lifted the camera and looked critically at the playback screen. She frowned. "I need my other lens. I'm doing photo montages of faces. Do you mind if I mix up parts of your face with parts of other people's faces?"

"That is a very disturbing thought," said Maggie. "No, really! Stop!" She started laughing again as Lena took a photograph of her chin. "I have a zit on my chin! You may *not* photograph that!" She put her hand up to cover the lens.

"I won't show it to anyone. I promise! I'm very respectful of my subjects." Lena flashed through the shots on her camera screen again, smiling at a few. Then she looked at Maggie, who must have had a strange look on her face. "Yikes! Am I being too forward? I tend to do that. Especially with people I like."

Maggie was surprised. Who talked like this? Especially with someone they'd just met? Hoping to redirect the conversation, she said, "Hey, thanks for saying you peed in your pants at lunch. I mean—not that you peed in your pants at lunch but that . . . you know what I mean." Lena was laughing. Maggie decided to change the subject again. "Can I take a picture of you?"

"Absolutely!" said Lena. "I *love* having my picture taken."

Maggie took the camera and snapped a photo of Lena smiling, but when Lena looked at it, she shook her head. "Too ordinary," she said. "Try taking one from a weird angle. Like in a way that no one has ever taken a photo before."

So Maggie snapped a picture of Lena's back, then one of her toes (all ten of them lined up in a row), then one of her armpit.

"These are awesome!" Lena jumped in excitement, looking at the playback of the photos on the camera's screen. "You've got talent, Maggie Gallagher!"

They had reached the top of the hill. "This is my house," said Maggie, handing back the camera.

Lena took the camera from her and smiled. "Can I come in?" She ruffled her hand through her pixie cut, making the sweaty ends stand up in spikes. Maggie hesitated.

"Sorry!" said Lena. "Too forward again. Such a bad habit!"

Maggie laughed. "No, it's okay." *Weird, but okay,* she thought. She imagined Lena meeting Grandpop, who could be downright rude, and her mother, who—that was a whole other mess. Maggie worried that Lena wouldn't think she was so great after meeting her family. But today was Monday, and that was the day that Maggie's grandfather went to the medical center for his weekly monitoring. A handicapped-accessible van picked him up at one o'clock. And her mother probably wouldn't be home until dinnertime. Still, maybe it would be better to go to Lena's house. "Where do you live?" asked Maggie.

Lena pointed down the road. "We're renting a house at the end of 2½ Street. The last one, actually."

"Oh," said Maggie. There were a lot of ramshackle houses in Odawahaka, but 2½ Street was one of the shaggiest roads in town. It wasn't even an actual road, just sort of a half-paved cow path that meandered off 2nd Street at an odd angle, crossed over 1st Street, and then dead-ended by the river. There were a few rusty trailer homes and a couple of abandoned houses. Maggie wondered if Lena's house was the sagging one that sat way up at the top of a long flight of crumbling stairs. The one that kids steered clear of on Halloween night. "Well, sure, come on in. Do you want a Moxie or something?"

"You know what?" Lena asked dramatically, her eyes growing wide. "I've never had a Moxie. But it's the *only* drink people talk about in this town!"

"Yeah," said Maggie, feeling a little embarrassed. "People here really love their Moxie. It's kind of like loving the losing home team. Or a particularly obnoxious uncle."

"Well, if you're offering, then the answer is yes!" said Lena.

They walked into the kitchen, and Maggie handed Lena a cold soda and a Keebler Vienna Fingers cookie, then grabbed a glass of milk and a cookie for herself. Lena opened the bottle and took a big swig.

"Whoa!" she said, holding the bottle away from her.

"I know, right?" said Maggie. "That's everyone's first response. But just give it a minute. And then take another sip."

Lena waited, swallowed another slug of soda, said nothing, and then took a third gulp. "It's growing on me," she admitted.

"Yep," said Maggie. "That's Moxie. By the time you finish the bottle, you'll either love it or hate it. There's no middle ground."

"Can I see your room?" asked Lena, raising the bottle to her lips again.

Um. "Okay," said Maggie. She was running through a quick inventory of everything she'd left out. "There's kind of a mess on the floor. . . ."

"I don't care!" said Lena, taking a picture of a refrigerator magnet shaped like the state of Pennsylvania.

At the top of the stairs, Lena ran her hand along the wall in the dim hallway. "Ooh! Cool wallpaper!"

"I hate it," said Maggie flatly. The wallpaper was faded and dull, a repeating pattern of Little Boy Blue asleep under the haystack, the sheep in the meadow, the cow in the corn. "Pretty much, I hate everything in this house."

Lena gave her a strange look, as if she were thinking very seriously about what Maggie had just said. "I *like* old things," she finally admitted, snapping a few close-ups of the wallpaper. "Old people. Old houses. Old photographs." Then she followed Maggie into her room. "Wow, you weren't kidding about a mess. You're worse than me! Which I thought was impossible!"

Lena took great pains to step carefully over the 127 vacuum cleaner parts that were laid out on the wooden floor of Maggie's small bedroom. "Are you fixing it? Whatever it is?"

"It's a vacuum cleaner. And it wasn't broken," said Maggie, biting into her cookie and settling on the bed. "I'm just deconstructing it and then reconstructing it. Helps me learn. And then I know what parts I've got on hand in case I need to fix something *else.*"

"Very cool," said Lena. "I'm not mechanical, but I like to construct, too. And I *love* to tear things apart." She took a whole series of close-ups of the small metal parts of the old vacuum cleaner. "I can use these," she muttered to herself as she worked.

When Lena stood up, she turned and studied Maggie's desk. "Who's that?" She was pointing to an old photograph taped to Maggie's computer screen.

Maggie paused, mid-bite.

"That's my dad," she said.

In the picture, he was standing on an endless expanse of green grass, with one hand on his hip and the other arm pretending to lean casually against a white stone building that was actually far in the background. The building looked like something out of ancient Rome or Greece, with ten massive columns stretching skyward and an enormous dome sitting on top. Her father was smiling from ear to ear, the first day of his freshman year at college.

Lena moved in for a closer look. "No way! He's so young!"

"It's an old picture. He went to MIT, which is"— Maggie waved her hand in an attempt to express the magnitude of the Massachusetts Institute of

Technology—"the mecca of engineering. I'm going to go there when I graduate from high school."

"Ooh, it's really hard to get into, isn't it? Super-elite East Coast school, yah?"

"Twenty thousand kids apply every year and only fifteen hundred get in. So, yeah, pretty hard. But I'm going to do it."

"Good for you!" said Lena. "I know you can."

Maggie was surprised by this response. Her mother always reminded her not to get her hopes up. *I just don't want you to be disappointed.* But here was Lena, who had only just met her, saying she believed in Maggie and her dreams.

"You're smart enough," said Lena. "And your dad can help, right?"

That brought Maggie back down to earth. "No. He's dead. He died before I was born. That's why it's such an old picture. He was really young."

"Oh, Maggie." Lena looked at her from across the room. "That's so sad. I'm really sorry."

"It was a long time ago. I don't even think about him anymore." Which wasn't even close to the truth. Maggie thought about her father every day. And she missed him with an aching that was sometimes overwhelming, which was strange since she'd never known him. But that's how it was. She even imagined his voice speaking to her: giving advice and helping her with problems. She supposed that was weird, but it brought her comfort.

Lena bent down and examined the photograph carefully. "It's incredible how much you two are alike." She snapped a picture. "Almost photographic."

That made Maggie smile. Her mother sometimes said that, too, *You're just like your father*, but never in a good way.

Lena's eyes continued to travel around the room, noticing the posters. "Wait! I'm sensing a theme!" She pointed to each poster. "Margaret Thatcher. Margaret Meade. Princess Margaret. Maggie Smith."

Maggie smiled. Emily and Allie had been in her room hundreds of times and never made the connection between the posters and Maggie's name. Lena, though, seemed to scoop up everything with her eyes—maybe because she was a photographer.

"I'm going to find you a poster of Margaret Bourke-White," said Lena. "Best photographer ever. What's this one?" She pointed to a movie poster from the 1950s.

Maggie felt hot and uncomfortable. "Nothing," she said. She stood up quickly, accidentally kicking the wheel assembly of the vacuum cleaner so that it rolled under the bed.

Don't forget the Fifth Commandment in the Hacker's Bible, whispered her father in her ear. *"No one should ever know."*

Maggie was frantically reaching under the bed to retrieve the wheel assembly. Her hand brushed against the box she kept hidden there.

"I saw this movie once," said Lena slowly, still staring at the poster. "I watched it with my dad. He likes old movies."

"It doesn't have anything to do with my name. It's just a dumb old poster. I don't even remember why I have it." Maggie's hand finally closed on the wheel assembly, and she placed it back where it belonged. The thought banged in her brain: she'd messed up.

Lena read the movie title slowly out loud. *"The Mouse That Roared."* She slapped her hand on her forehead. "I should have figured it out sooner!" She turned to Maggie. "'Roar!' On the tennis balls. On the balloons. *The Mouse That Roared! Du-u-uh!"*

She smiled as if she'd just received the happiest news possible. "And the best, best, best part is that it's *you*. You're the Mouse."

She lifted her camera to her eye and snapped a photo of Maggie's flabbergasted face. Later, Lena would title that picture *Caught in the Act*.

56

EIGHT

THERE WAS A LOT TO TELL. One cookie apiece wasn't enough. The girls returned to the kitchen, where Maggie pulled down the entire package of Vienna Fingers then poured herself a glass of milk. They both sat down at the kitchen table.

"What I want to know first," said Lena, stacking up a pile of six cookies and then prying apart one to lick the vanilla cream inside, "is why did you do it?"

Maggie gave her a funny look. "Why? You don't want to know *how?*"

How was where Maggie always started. *How can I build a long-range remote control so that I can turn off the noisy neighbor's TV from my bedroom? How can I add a fuel booster to the engine of Mom's fifteen-year-old Corolla so she'll get an extra mile to the gallon? How can I add stress supports to the front porch so the whole roof doesn't cave in?* Life was a series of questions, and for Maggie they all began with *how.* She was an engineer, through and through.

"Well, yes," said Lena, biting loudly into the crunchy cookie part. "I want to know that, too, but . . . okay, how? How did you get all the tennis balls in the locker?"

"It's an old hacker's trick," said Maggie. "You use a piece of cardboard to create a barrier, pile all the balls inside the space, close the locker door as much as possible, and then slowly slide the cardboard out and quickly latch the door. The next person who opens the door—gets buried."

Lena nodded seriously. "Brilliant. Simple, but brilliant." She pried apart another cookie. "And where'd you get all the race cars?"

"A website. Nothing clever there."

"But what about the balloons in the rotunda and the sheet? How did you get that to stay in place?"

"Tension clips," said Maggie. "Tension clips are great for suspending anything that's light." Maggie carried her empty glass to the sink. She was finished eating, but Lena looked like she might polish off the entire package of cookies.

"But how did you make it so that no one *noticed* the balloons up there? No one saw them, until the mouse parachuted down. It's like they were invisible and every-one was walking right under them."

Maggie smiled. "*That* is human nature. People almost never look up. Did you know that? They've done scientific studies. Humans tend to look mid-level or down—especially in high-stress situations like the first day of school."

"And what about getting *into* the school?" asked Lena. "When did you do that? And how?"

Nightwork, Maggie thought. It was the term that hackers used for setting up their hacks under the cover of darkness. There was a joke in one of her father's notebooks: *Nightwork. It's good work if you can get it. And get out.*

"I'll just say this," said Maggie, smiling as she thought of her father. "There's always a way in, if you look hard enough. And I'm not a person who needs a lot of sleep."

Lena shook her head in admiration. "You're incred-ible. Ninja incredible." Slowly, she chewed on her cookie, then asked, "So, how did you get the mouse to drop down at exactly the right moment?"

A sour expression came over Maggie's face. "That was a mistake. A miscalculation." She tapped her fin-gers on the countertop in irritation. "I had the mouse on a timer, and it was supposed to drop down at the end of the day. Sort of a celebration for the end of the first day of school. But timers are tricky. They're mechanical, so just about anything can throw them off. And I don't always have the best parts to work with." She thought of the guts of the vacuum cleaner on the floor in her bedroom. "So it malfunctioned."

"But it was *great* the way it worked!" said Lena. "Sometimes happy accidents happen in art. And sometimes they happen with timers, too!"

Maggie shook her head. "Not in hacking. Hacking is science. It's meant to be precise. In hacking, timing is everything."

"Hacking?" asked Lena slowly. "Isn't that like where criminals steal computer data and ruin people's lives?"

Maggie groaned. "That's *not* what hacking is. I wish people would stop getting that wrong. Hacking means pulling off a prank with style. Something that requires intelligence and technical know-how and daring. Look: a *prank* is when you flatten someone's car tires. Ha-ha. A *hack* is when you disassemble, transport, and then reassemble a full-size police car on the dome of a building, one hundred and fifty feet in the air. My dad did that when he was at MIT. *He* was a hacker. Better than anybody. Ever."

"Wow! A police car on top of a building? Let me guess: he didn't need a lot of sleep, either."

"The first person to notice the car was a jogger, just before sunrise. The red and blue lights on top of the car were flashing, and there was a dummy dressed up like a police officer at the wheel with a half-eaten box of doughnuts. There was even a ticket on the windshield: 'No permit for this location.' *That* was a hack."

"I wish I could have seen it," said Lena.

"I have a photo. It made it into newspapers all over the world, it was *that* incredible."

"You have a photo? Where?"

Maggie froze, her mouth slightly open. She could feel one cookie crumb still clinging to her lower lip, and she hurried to brush it off. A long chain of if-then statements ran through her mind: *If* she showed Lena the picture, *then* she would have to show her the box hidden under her bed. *If* she showed her the box, *then* Lena would see the Hacker's Bible. *If* Lena saw the Hacker's Bible, *then* she would enter the private world that belonged to Maggie and her father alone. She stood up from her chair and walked over to the sink to get a drink of water, turning her back on Lena.

"Oh, I don't even know where it is," she said, as if it was the littlest of things, something so small it could be lost and forgotten. She gulped the water, then rinsed the glass and put it in the drying rack. When she turned back to face Lena, she hoped she had wiped every emotion from her face.

Lena looked at her. A quiet moment passed between them. Maggie had the same uncomfortable feeling she'd had when they were in her room: that Lena saw everything. She was a sponge that soaked up everything. Nothing seemed to get by her. There was no place to hide.

Well, maybe one place.

"Do you want to see my secret laboratory?" asked Maggie, hoping to distract Lena and bring back the fun they'd been having.

"Of course!" said Lena, scooping up her remaining cookies and grabbing three more from the package.

The two girls headed downstairs.

Maggie was lucky that Grandpop's house even had a basement. A lot of the houses in Odawahaka didn't because of the hard bedrock that edged up from the Susquehanna River into the surrounding hills. But more than a hundred years ago, Grandpop's great-grandfather had blasted through the rock with dynamite and smashed out a proper basement. (Perhaps the love of a good explosion had seeped into

Maggie's bones from that first big bang.)

Lena was impressed by the rickety staircase. "It looks like something out of a horror movie! Like it could collapse at any minute! I love it!"

When they were finally standing on the dirt floor, Lena began to *ooh* and *aah* about the blasted rock walls of the basement. She studied one bare face of the wall. "Watch this!" she said, putting her camera on a nearby workbench. In five seconds, she had climbed up the wall, grabbing hold of the jutting rock and finding toeholds in the smallest outcroppings and crevices. She tapped the ceiling, then dropped back down. The whole stunt had taken less than ten seconds.

"How did you do that?" asked Maggie, wondering if she'd really just seen Lena climb the wall like a spider.

"I have freaky long arms. Totally out of proportion with the rest of my body. See!" Maggie looked. Lena's arms were kind of long. Maggie wasn't sure if she should compliment her or insist it wasn't true. "I used to compete."

"There are contests for long arms?" Maggie's eyes grew wide. She would never want to call attention to herself like that.

"No!" Lena laughed. "Rock climbing, goofus! I have mad upper-body strength. I'm basically an orangutan."

She reached for her camera. "Whoa! What is this?"

Lena was staring at Grandpop's pile of auto parts, scavenged and scrapped when he was still young and worked on muscle cars—Barracudas and Camaros and GTOs. Maggie once estimated that there were close to two thousand pieces, from gas pedals to spark plugs.

"That," said Maggie, making a quick calculation and deciding to take a chance, "is how I fund this whole operation."

Maggie took Lena back up to her room. On her computer, she called up a webpage: a classy-looking site called Vinnie's Vintage Auto Parts, complete with photographs of the inventory, a search field with sortable results, e-commerce capability, and hundreds of positive customer reviews.

"That's me," said Maggie. "I'm Vinnie. I identify the parts from the basement; clean, fix, refurbish them; take pictures; then post the photos on the website. I've got over five hundred parts posted right now. And no matter how many I sell, Grandpop's pile never seems to get smaller!"

"Who writes the reviews?" asked Lena.

"They're real! All of them," said Maggie. "And I get five stars every time. I'm not kidding. There are thousands of people all over the country who rebuild muscle cars, and *they love Vinnie.* He never disappoints! The site is incredibly popular. And I'm not just saying that."

"Where does the money go?" asked Lena, scrolling through the website.

"Directly into my bank account. Plus"—she dropped her voice, even though they were alone in the house—"I have a credit card. It wasn't even hard to get."

"Maggie Gallagher, you are nothing but trouble!" said Lena, hugging her enthusiastically with her freakishly long arms. It was obvious from the look on Lena's face that there was no higher compliment in her book. "You are the perfect partner in crime!"

Maggie felt the same way: that she and Lena fit together. They were different from each other—there was no denying that—but they both had a spark of curiosity that was decidedly lacking in Odawahaka.

And they liked to break rules.

All her life, Maggie had felt she didn't fit in, especially with her father's voice pointing out the many ways she was different. Maybe that was why she often felt alone, even when she was hanging out with Allie and Emily. It was kind of isolating to feel that the person you were most closely attuned to was someone who had died before you were even born.

Maggie didn't mind being different.

But it might be nice to be different with Lena.

"Okay," said Lena. "You've explained the *how*—and beautifully, I might add. Now I want to know *why*. But first I want another Moxie."

Lena linked arms with Maggie (which was a little awkward because of the extreme difference in their heights), and they walked downstairs, bumping the whole way, which just made them laugh all the harder. Maggie handed Lena a soda, slightly worried that her grandfather would notice that two bottles were gone. They wandered out to the front porch in search of a cooling breeze in the late afternoon and sat on the porch swing. Maggie pulled her feet up, but Lena's long legs were perfect for pushing the swing slowly back and forth. It was still blazingly hot, and Maggie knotted her hair on top of her head with a pencil and one of Grand-pop's "scratching sticks."

"So. Why?" asked Lena, taking a sip of her soda. "Why did you do that amazing hack?"

"Just because," said Maggie. She was using her fingers to rake stray curls off her face, hoping her sweat would make them stick to the sides of her head. A fly buzzed and landed. Buzzed and landed. "Hacking is one of those just-because things. You do it to see if you can do it. And then once you know you can do it, you move on to the next hack. It's a puzzle. A game. There's no reason. *Hackito, ergo sum.* I hack, therefore I am." Her dad had written that in one of his notebooks.

"Ye-e-e-s," said Lena. "But there *could* be a reason. That hack today made a lot of people happy."

"And *someone* incredibly unhappy!" said Maggie. They both laughed, thinking of Principal Shute and his baseball bat.

"Seriously," said Lena. "He's kind of wacko, don't you think? Stretched a little tight? Ready to snap?"

"My dad would say, 'A few too many coils in his spring.'" She had read that phrase a few times in her father's notebooks.

"Exactly. So maybe we should loosen him a bit?" said Lena. "Wait. I'm going to burp." They sat in silence for ten seconds. "False alarm."

But alarms were going off in Maggie's head. *We?* Was Lena suggesting the two of them *hack* together? Where did *that* come from?

Is she serious? asked Maggie's father.

When Maggie had told Lena the details of that morning's epic hack, she hadn't considered that she was opening a door to hacking. She hadn't intended to invite Lena into that part of her life. Maggie had always hacked with her father. The notebooks hidden in the box under her bed were filled with his instructions, detailed diagrams, follow-up notes, and running commentary. (*Use thick rope. Thin rope frays when dragged over the edge of a building. . . . Never forget duct tape. It will save your life.* And most important: *All Tech Men carry batteries.*) They were a team, Maggie and her father, and Maggie didn't feel alone when she was hacking with him.

Lena tapped the top of her Moxie bottle with her palm, making that eerie deep-well sound. "Clearly Principal Shute can't stand fun of any kind," she said. "So if our goal is to bring fun to Oda M, thereby driving Principal Shute a little crazy—"

Hang on! shouted her dad.

"Wait!" said Maggie. "I never said—" She grew flustered. Hacking was the one thing on earth that belonged to her and her dad. She couldn't lose that. She absolutely couldn't. In horror, she realized that tears were starting to sting her eyes.

"Oh no! What did I do?" asked Lena, putting her soda on the table. "I'm so sorry. I'm making you cry. I didn't mean to, Maggie. Whatever I said, I take it right back. A hundred times."

Maggie wiped her nose with the edge of her T-shirt. (Duct tape was useless in a situation like this.) "No. It's stupid! I don't even know why I'm crying. It's just that, in my head . . . This is really hard to explain, and you're probably going to think I'm completely crazy. But in my head . . . I hack with my dad."

Lena nodded. "And I just barged in," she said. "Like a giant turtle."

Maggie laughed. "I never cry," she said, which was mostly true. She worked hard to keep the really sad stuff out of her mind.

"I cry all the time," said Lena. "I cry when I hear a sad story. I cry if I find a dead squirrel. Last week, I cried when we were out of milk." She straightened up. "But the hacking thing. That's all yours. And your dad's. Message received!"

"No," said Maggie. "That's the thing. I think that's the thing that's making me cry." And she felt the tears start to come again. Lena wiggled closer to her on the swing. "I think . . . I think it would be really . . . fun . . . to hack with you."

And that's when Lena burped. One of the longest, loudest burps Maggie had ever heard in her life. It was prodigious.

"Excuse me!" said Lena. "Didn't see that coming!"

Maggie stared at her, stunned. "What did you just say?" It was what her father always said, what he had written dozens of times in his notebooks.

"I said, 'Excuse me!'" said Lena. "I'm rude, but I'm not usually that rude!"

Maggie felt a strange shiver run up her spine. It was as though her father had spoken out loud—but through someone else. And she was pretty sure he was saying it was okay.

Lena picked up the bottle of soda and stared at it. "Clearly, what this girl needs is a little less Moxie!"

"You know what Mrs. Dornbusch would say to that?" asked Maggie. Both girls shouted: "I. Don't. Care!"

"I know what let's do!" said Lena, jumping up from the porch swing. "Let's go around town and take pictures of all the best places in Odawahaka. You can be my tour guide."

"There are no 'best places' in Odawahaka!" said Maggie. Lena looked at her expectantly. "No, I'm serious. There is absolutely nothing to see or do in this town."

But in the end, Lena convinced her to walk around, and as they walked, they came across the World War II tank on Main Street and the 1775 Friends Meetinghouse on South Street and the old steam engines and railroad cars on Pine Street and the deserted, once elegant Opera House on the corner of 4th and Mill. They were able to find four different cars that displayed the Moxie bumper sticker. And finally, they ended up down by the river, where the slow-moving water flowed by, as it had for millions of years. At each place they stopped, Lena took a picture of Maggie. And in each picture, Maggie was smiling.

NINE

AFTER SAYING GOOD-BYE TO LENA, MAGGIE climbed the hill until she reached her house at the very top of 3rd Street where it intersected with North on the edge of town. Standing outside the metal gate, she could see the whole of Odawahaka spread out like a tablecloth. There was the black-capped bell tower of St. John's Church. And there was the bridge that carried people across the river and away from the town. Maggie's grandfather liked to say that if the brake on his wheelchair ever gave way, he'd find himself halfway to hell in a hurry.

The light was just starting to dim, and Maggie wondered if her mother was home and had already fed Grandpop his dinner or if that chore would fall to her, as it often did. She stopped for a minute to look up at the purple darkness of the hill that loomed over the town, and then across the street and down a little ways to her favorite house in Odawahaka.

The house was broad, with a clean wooden porch that reached comfortably from one end to the other. The wooden clapboards were olive green, and the shutters that neatly framed each six-paned window were a deeper green. The trim was a creamy white that made Maggie think of buttermilk. It was one of the oldest houses in town, but it looked fresh and lovely, as if it had just been dressed for a party. When she was little, Maggie called it the Golden House.

She thought of the hundreds of times she'd been inside that house, and how long it had been since she had last set foot even in the yard. Almost five years, but she still remembered the butler's pantry off the kitchen, the lace curtains in the living room, the smell of chicken roasting in the oven, and the pitcher of pink lemonade that was set on a special tea cart every afternoon in the summer. You could take as many glasses as you wanted. You didn't even have to ask. And Maggie remembered Kayla's mother calling her "sweetheart" and "honey." Until she didn't.

Maggie pushed open the chain-link gate that fenced in her own small yard, noticing that her mother's car was parked in the narrow, concrete-covered space alongside the house. When she walked in, Grandpop was already on the warpath.

"I don't want macaroni again," he complained. "And it doesn't matter what fancy name you give it. It's still macaroni, and I'm sick of it. I swear, I'll start speaking Italian at this rate!"

Maggie could hear the creak of his wheelchair as he strained against it. By the end of the day, his body ached and his mood was fast heading south. She heard the bang of a casserole dish in the oven, and her mother said something in response that Maggie couldn't make out.

"Well, that's not my fault, now is it?" replied her grandfather.

"Dad," Maggie's mother's weary voice said. "I'm just too tired to get into it." There was the sound of ice in a glass, and then the steady *glug, glug* of something being poured from a bottle and the bottle being set down hard on the countertop. Then Maggie heard the pop of a soda can and the fizz and splash of the soda being poured over the ice.

"Too tired, too tired," said Maggie's grandfather. "If I had a nickel for every time you said that, Janey . . ."

"We'd be eating nickels for dinner," said Maggie's mother, taking a long swallow of her drink. "And then you'd complain that you're sick of eating nickels and would I please make a nice macaroni dish for a change."

"Very funny. Now, your mother was—"

"Yes. We all remember," said Maggie's mother. "Mom was an amazing cook. Could make a banquet out of shoe leather and nails." Maggie walked into the kitchen. Her mother stopped short, then added more softly, "And we all miss her. Right, Boo?" Maggie's mother looked at Maggie, then sat down heavily at the kitchen table and took another long drink.

Maggie didn't say anything. She'd been so young when Grandmom had died that it was hard to be sure of any of her memories.

Grandpop jerked his chair around, maneuvering in the tight space. "Call me when dinner's ready," he said, wheeling himself into the living room. They heard the TV blaze to life as one of Grandpop's favorite reality shows came on.

"How was school?" her mother asked, but Maggie could tell that her thoughts were a thousand miles away.

"Fine. How was school for you?" Maggie's mother taught biology at a small community college an hour away. Grandpop claimed her salary was hardly worth what she spent on gas to get to and from work.

"Dandy," she said, fishing ice out of her drink. "They assigned me another class, but they're not giving me more money to teach it." She raised her glass. "All hail Academia!"

Maggie filled a glass with water and drank it down. All that walking with Lena had left her feeling dehydrated and empty. Dried up like the husk of a fly. "Mom?" she asked, looking out the window. "Were you a suck-up?"

"What? What kind of a thing is that to ask?" Her mother refilled her glass.

"I just wondered what kind of a kid you were when you were my age."

Her mother looked at her suspiciously. "I was a good student. Diligent. Some things didn't come easily to me, and I had to work hard in those subjects. And I followed the rules. I didn't take shortcuts and I didn't cause trouble. Maybe that's what you mean by 'suck-up.'"

"But you were smart. You graduated the top of your class," said Maggie.

"I was a certain kind of smart. You'll understand when you're older."

"You were the Golden Girl," whispered Maggie.

"Everyone in town says so."

"Maybe that's how it looked to them," said Maggie's mother, swirling the ice in her drink before taking another gulp. "But it didn't come easy. Not like it does for you."

"Or Dad?" Maggie stopped breathing. Silence held the room captive. Her mother stared down into her drink. In the quiet, Maggie could hear a piece of ice melt and then fall.

"Everything was easy for him," said her mother. "He made it all look like a game."

"Did he—"

"Maggie!" said her mother, standing up. "I have hours of grading to do, and an early faculty meeting in the morning."

Maggie knew only the bare outline of her father's story. Her parents had married right after college and were living in Cambridge, Massachusetts. Her father had plans to get his PhD in electrical engineering, and Maggie's mother had just finished her master's degree in biology. They were the best of the best. Their whole future lay in front of them, with the happy news of a baby on the way. And then the car accident that killed Maggie's father, and the setting of the story shifted to Odawahaka, where Maggie's life began.

Maggie thought of Mrs. Dornbusch's comment about her mother. *What a waste.* She would never understand that part of the story, but she knew with all the certainty of her heart that she was *not* going to end up like her mother.

"We could still leave," said Maggie quietly. Then with more urgency, "Go back East. You could get a better job. I would . . ." She wasn't even quite sure how to finish that sentence. Be happy? Belong? Be closer to Dad, who was buried in a cemetery next to a river like the one that ran through their town? Or at least that's how Maggie always imagined it. That somehow the Susquehanna met up with the Charles, and there was a way to get from *here* to *there*. Even though the maps proved her wrong.

"Maggie," pleaded her mother, and the strain and exhaustion made her voice rise. "You have no idea how big the world is. For every hometown girl who's the Smart One, there are thousands more. You just get lost in them. It's better to stay home." She brushed an invisible crumb off the table. "Where it's safe."

"But we could—"

"Enough." Her mother tucked the bottle under her arm, then picked up her worn leather satchel stuffed with student lab reports. "I've got grading to do. Can you take the casserole out of the oven when the timer goes off and serve it to Grandpop?" She walked out of the kitchen, brushing past Maggie but not slowing down, even to drop a kiss on her head.

Grading papers, thought Maggie. *Right.*

All the shine had worn off the afternoon. What did it matter that there was a new girl in town? It was the same Odawahaka, and Maggie wasn't going anywhere soon. What would really change?

Maggie checked the timer, then went upstairs to her own room, carefully closing the door behind her. In her mother's bedroom, she could hear the TV turned on low. Maggie knelt down and pulled the hidden box out from under her bed.

The box was roughly the size of a small suitcase and had been repaired so many times over the years that it was made more of duct tape than cardboard. Maggie pulled off the lid and removed the twenty spiral-bound notebooks that took up most of the space inside. The top notebook had a flimsy, worn black cover. Scratched into the surface, as if with the cap of a cheap ballpoint pen, were the words *The Hacker's Bible.* Maggie turned to the first page. In her father's neat, mechanical writing were the Ten Commandments:

1. BE ORIGINAL. IF YOU CAN'T BE ORIGINAL, JUST STAY HOME AND WATCH TV.

2. BE SAFE. IF YOU GET HURT, YOU'VE FAILED.

3. DON'T DESTROY ANYTHING THAT DOESN'T BELONG TO YOU. DESTRUCTION = FAILURE.

4. NEVER STEAL. IF YOU NEED TO BORROW SOMETHING, LEAVE A NOTE BEHIND THAT EXPLAINS WHEN AND HOW YOU WILL RETURN THE BORROWED ITEM.

5. DON'T BRAG. HACKING IS MEANT TO BE ANONYMOUS; NO ONE SHOULD EVER KNOW WHO PULLED OFF A HACK.

6. NEVER HACK ALONE. IT ISN'T SAFE. (SEE SECOND COMMANDMENT)

7. DON'T GET CAUGHT. BUT IF YOU DO GET CAUGHT, DON'T EMBARRASS YOURSELF BY DENIAL.

8. LEAVE DETAILED INSTRUCTIONS FOR HOW TO DISASSEMBLE A HACK SAFELY, AND LEAVE A SITE IN BETTER SHAPE THAN YOU FOUND IT.

9. DURING SETUP, DON'T RAISE OR DROP THINGS FROM HIGH PLACES WITHOUT GROUND SUPERVISION. THIS INCLUDES CARS, DESKS, BORROWED UNIVERSITY PROPERTY, TOOLS, TOILETS, AND FELLOW HACKERS.

10. SHARE YOUR KNOWLEDGE WITH OTHERS. AND DON'T WASTE YOUR LIFE WATCHING TV.

The rest of the notebooks were crammed with Maggie's father's notes on every hack he and his hacking crew (the Gamma Gamma Heys) had executed at MIT. There was the time the Gamma Gamma Heys completely wallpapered over the door to the new president's office so that he couldn't find it on his first day of work. There was the time they put a twenty-foot model of the *Starship Enterprise* in the lobby of Building 10. There was the time they created a life-size replica of an MIT dorm room (complete with a bed, a desk, a working lamp, and an alarm clock that couldn't be turned off) and positioned it on the frozen Charles River. And then there was the police car perched atop the Great Dome. Each hack more impossible to figure out than the last.

But in these notebooks were the complete instructions, down to the gauge of the wire, the thickness of the rip cord, the recipe for the heat-resistant glue. There were even notes on how to make small quantities of proto–rocket fuel.

The margins were filled with her father's comments. He was hypercritical of anyone who couldn't keep up with him (*Never let Griggs near a fuse box again*), hard on himself (*stupid, stupid, stupid*), and always exploring new possibilities (*Series-connected? Test tomorrow using house blender*). He liked to joke. In one margin, he had doodled a picture of himself with his wild and curly hair on fire. The caption read, *Where there's smoke, there's Tech Men hacking.*

Maggie had read these comments so many times that it was as if some version of her father lived in her brain. And the conversation just went on and on.

She put aside the notebooks and shuffled through the remaining contents of the box: half a dozen photographs, a handful of press clippings, a letter from the dean pleading with the Gamma Gamma Heys to "show restraint" during Parents' Weekend, her father's student ID card, a key, a standard-issue MIT baseball cap that someone had embellished with the embroidered words *Mouse In Training.* Maggie sifted through each item, always hoping that she had somehow missed something. That there would be some new piece of her father to hold in her hands.

When she reached the bottom and the box was empty, she carefully returned everything as it had been, then slid the box under her bed. She could hear the kitchen timer going off downstairs. She scrambled to her feet, but not before her grandfather could start his grousing.

"I'm coming! I'm coming already!" shouted Maggie. The T-shirt slogan *Dada Is My Daddy* suddenly flashed in her brain, and she laughed for a second, trying to imagine explaining Dadaism to Grandpop.

Just before she left her room she heard the ping of an email landing in her in-box. As if by telepathy, the email had a one-word subject line: *DADA!* Maggie opened it; there was no message, just a picture of the *Mona Lisa* with the face of Mrs. Dornbusch expertly Photoshopped over it. It looked like it could be an actual painting hanging in a museum. The effect was incredibly eerie.

Maggie stared at the image. Downstairs the TV was blaring. In her mother's room, the TV was humming. But here, in this little space she'd carved out for herself, Dada lived.

She allowed herself one more moment in the glow of the computer's screen, then hurried downstairs to take the casserole out of the oven.

Even with a casserole, timing mattered.

TEN

OF COURSE MAGGIE EMAILED LENA BACK later that evening to tell her how much she loved the "Mona Dornbusch" painting, and then Lena emailed *her* back, and then Maggie emailed *her* back . . . and then here they were the next morning: sneaking into the empty school two hours before the school day began.

It was only the second day of the school year, and most sixth graders were still in bed, ignoring their parents' pleas to *"Get up!"* But Maggie and Lena were creeping around the rear of the school. Both girls had backpacks, but Maggie also carried her old Little Mermaid insulated lunch pack from first grade. It held dry ice and two small glass bottles filled with a clear liquid. By the look and the smell of it, it could have been water. But it wasn't water.

"Aren't you afraid it's going to explode?" asked Lena. Maggie had described the volatile results of what would happen if even a feather touched the solution.

"Nope, it's safe. As long as we keep it cold and dark and wet." The chemical compound she had made was floating safely in a slosh of ammonia. It was completely stable—until the ammonia evaporated.

"How do you even know about this door?" asked Lena as Maggie pushed aside the overgrown branches of a neglected buttonwood bush to reveal a rusted metal entrance.

"I make it my business to know every way in and every way out. When you hack, you have to know your routes."

"Ha! Roots!" said Lena, pointing at the bush, which had just slapped her in the face as if it were alive. There was a scraggly daisy plant at the foot of the bush. Lena snapped off a single flower and tucked it into the buttonhole of her denim jacket.

That's right, whispered Maggie's father. *Always know your entrances and exits. . . .* Maggie could tell that her father was annoyed that there was a third member of their hacking team, but she didn't have time to dwell on negatives. They were about to re-create the *original* MIT hack, and it involved *explosions.* What could be better?

Back in the 1870s, the first MIT hackers occasionally sprinkled nitrogen triiodide on the gymnasium floor so that students practicing their military drills had a little extra *snap*, *crackle*, and *pop* to their routine assembly. It was harmless, but inevitably led to chaos—it's hard to keep marching in a straight line when the floor is exploding beneath your feet.

That's what Lena had loved about the idea of adding some unexpected zip to gym class. Chaos when you least expected it. A surprise in the most familiar of places. A beard on the *Mona Lisa*. A urinal on display in a museum. "We're modern-day Dadaists," she had said to Maggie.

Whatever. Maggie just loved explosions.

Lena stepped back in fear when Maggie tried to hand her the lunch pack. "It's safe!" promised Maggie, turning her attention to the rusted-shut door. "Trust me." But Lena set the lunch pack carefully on the ground as soon as it was handed to her.

"It isn't locked?" asked Lena as Maggie lifted up on the door handle.

"Nope," said Maggie, pushing with her hip in just the right spot. "Mr. Fetterholf, the custodian, thinks it is, because it's jammed. I could fix it—it just needs its hinges readjusted and a good cleaning and oiling—but it's actually pretty useful to have a secret door that no one else knows. One time last year, I forgot my homework over the weekend, and this door totally saved my butt." Maggie pushed again. It was tricky, finding exactly the right spot.

"But there isn't an alarm system? Or surveillance cameras?"

Maggie stopped and looked at her. "Are you kidding? This is Oda M! We barely have lightbulbs! Believe me: there are no surveillance cameras!"

Maggie hit the door one more time with her hip. The rusted and forgotten door groaned as it opened into the cavernous old gym. Maggie picked up the lunch pack and hurried inside with Lena a cautious few steps behind.

There weren't real gym classes this year. Instead, the school fulfilled its state-mandated physical education requirement by assigning each teacher an hour's worth of "activity supervision" each week. Mr. Platt was eager to organize team games like capture the flag, kickball, and relay races. Mrs. Matlaw was planning to teach yoga and lead trust-building exercises. But Mrs. Dornbusch was old-school. They knew she would make them run laps or do calisthenics until the students flopped in exhaustion on the piles of wrestling mats that were soaked in fifty years of sweat. Lucky for the students, gym class was just one day a week, and today's session would be "taught" by Mrs. Matlaw. Maggie didn't expect that any trust would be built.

She set her backpack down on the gym floor and retrieved two pairs of safety gloves from its zippered front pocket.

"We're not going to make a mess of the gym, are we?" asked Lena. It was clear that Lena didn't like the thought of making more work for the school custodian.

"No," said Maggie. "We'll leave Mr. Fetterholf with clear instructions and a bottle of sodium thiosulfate. It'll wipe up the stains super easy. Or he could just wait, and the stains will disappear on their own."

The Third Commandment, whispered her father solemnly. *Don't destroy anything that doesn't belong to you. Destruction = Failure.*

"I know that!" said Maggie.

"Know what?" asked Lena.

Maggie closed her mouth. "Oh, nothing. I just sometimes talk to myself."

"Me too!" said Lena, laughing. "Especially when I'm painting. Two peas in a pod." And she put an arm around Maggie's shoulders and gave her a quick squeeze.

But they weren't two peas in a pod, and Maggie knew it. *I don't need your advice on everything,* she muttered inside her own head. She was used to talking out loud to her father during hacks. It was strange to have someone else along. Someone . . . real.

Hey! protested her father, but Maggie had decided to ignore him and was busy surveying the scene of the hack—the grand old gymnasium of Oda M.

"It's like a cathedral," whispered Lena, and Maggie knew just what she meant. The ceiling of the gym soared to fifty feet high, with a row of narrow windows at the top that allowed the early morning light to filter in. The air was still, and the quiet contained by the enormous space seemed that much more profound. It was like the calm of the forest on a snowy morning—the silence deepened by the vastness of the place.

Get a move on, urged her father.

Maggie and Lena looked straight up and were surprised by the complicated maze of air ducts, rafters, water pipes, beams, electrical wiring, trusses, supports, netting, vents, ropes, lights, and fans.

"Wow," said Lena. "It's like some kind of supercity with highways and factories and no road map."

"I didn't think it would be so high," Maggie worried.

"There are the ropes," said Lena. "Come on." She moved quickly to where the climbing ropes that hung from the ceiling were cleated to the wall. They needed only one, and so she chose the center rope and unhooked it. It hung down from a rafter in the ceiling, ending directly in the middle of the gym floor.

"It's too high!" said Maggie again. "We didn't *plan* for that height. You shouldn't do it. It isn't safe." She felt drops of sweat gather on her forehead and upper lip. Dampness seemed to suddenly appear out of nowhere under her arms. Just looking up at that height made her stomach drop down to her knees.

"Maggie!" said Lena. "This is the *easy* part. *You're* the one carrying explosives in your lunch box!"

"No!" said Maggie. "You can't do it!" Climbing *that* high hadn't been part of the plan.

Lena put a hand on each of Maggie's shoulders. "Breathe deep, Mags. This is what I'm good at. You're the planner. I'm the wing nut. This is what makes us such an awesome team."

Lena reached into her own backpack and chalked up her hands, then hooked the pack on her back and began to climb the rope hand over hand. She didn't even use her legs. Maggie couldn't believe someone could have that much strength in her arms. Lena made it to the top in less than a minute, flipped herself up, and sat on a rafter, catching her breath.

"I can't watch," said Maggie, feeling like she might

throw up. She stared down at the floor. "Just tell me what you're doing."

"It's so cool up here, Maggie. I wish you could see it."

"No way! Just do what you have to do." Then she heard the rapid-fire clicking of Lena's camera. Maggie wanted to scream. This was not how you hacked. "Come on!" she said urgently. "We don't have time for art!"

"There's always time for art," said Lena emphatically. "You might as well say there isn't time for life!" But she put her camera away and began to work. Once or twice, Maggie tried to look up to check on her friend, but just the sight of Lena sitting on the rafter so high above the ground made her feel nauseous. She imagined what her father would write about her in his notebook: *Useless when it comes to heights!*

A minute later, Lena was back on the ground, and Maggie breathed a huge sigh of relief. From here on out, everything was a piece of cake. They just had to handle small amounts of a highly sensitive contact explosive, preferably without blowing anything up.

They began at opposite corners of the large gym floor, staying within the lines marked by the basketball court.

"Remember," said Maggie, "just one drop, then move

down five feet, then one drop. All the way to the end of the row." The goal was to have the explosions just close enough so one would set off the next.

"The gloves feel weird," said Lena. "What if I drop the whole bottle?"

"Don't!" said Maggie emphatically. "Just don't. That's what hacking is. Planning and execution."

"What about the unexpected?" asked Lena. She had already completed her first row and was now working her way into the center of her next row. "That's what *art* is about."

And that's why hacking and art don't go together! said her father.

But for the first time, Maggie wondered if her father could be wrong about something. She thought she and Lena made a pretty good team.

Didn't see that coming, she whispered inside her head.

The girls met in the middle, back to back, each having finished half of the last row.

"Okay," said Maggie. "Now let's get out of here quickly, because as soon as the drops dry, the chemicals are highly unstable, and that's when the fun begins." They screwed the lids onto the bottles and took off their gloves, but in even that short amount of time, the droplets on the floor had . . . vanished.

"Which way?" asked Lena, looking down at the clean, dry floor.

"I'm pretty sure . . ." But now Maggie realized that she wasn't sure at all. They had laid down the droplets of nitrogen triiodide inside the faded lines that marked the perimeter of the basketball court so there were one hundred and thirty-five "hot spots" in all. Maggie had drawn a grid on paper, and the pattern was very clear in her head.

But here, on the actual surface of the scuffed gym floor, the pattern was not so clear. Especially since the drops had evaporated—which meant they were both invisible and ready to explode on contact. Even the touch of a feather would set them off. How had she not considered that it would be better to work from the center *out* instead of from the edges *in*? Planning was supposed to be her strong point!

Lena started to laugh.

"This is *not* funny!" insisted Maggie. How could Lena not understand that the whole hack would be ruined if they took a single wrong step? But then all of a sudden she realized that Lena *did* understand exactly that, and that was precisely the reason she was laughing. They had done all this planning and all this work, and now they were boxed in by their own hack!

Maggie cracked up. *This is why you should never hack alone*, she thought, recalling the Sixth Commandment. Forget about safety! It was just more fun.

"Okay," said Lena, gasping for air between howls of laughter. "This is what we're going to do. I'm going to pick a direction and just walk. And you're going to follow directly in my footsteps. If anything explodes, we'll stop and reassess. Okay?"

"Why should you go first?" asked Maggie, knowing that Lena was taking all the risk.

"Because I'm a person of faith, and the Universe will protect me. I believe!" And she set off with confident, careful strides in the direction of the gym's edge. Maggie sucked in a deep breath and followed.

Not one explosion. Maggie was both relieved and disappointed. What if she had mixed up the solution wrong? What if the entire hack was a dud?

"C'mon," said Lena. "Let's get out of here. We're tempting the Fates."

But as they quietly gathered up their backpacks and tiptoed toward the gym door, there was the sound of something softly hitting the floor. They turned to see the daisy that Lena had worn in the buttonhole of her jacket.

"Oh, Maggie!" said Lena. "I took it out when I was

up there because I didn't want it to fall by accident, and then I left it by mistake! It must have moved when I swung down on the rope."

"Well, we can't leave it there," said Maggie. "It's a flower in the middle of the gym floor! Mr. Fetterholf could come along and pick it up." The hack was *not* supposed to happen when Mr. Fetterholf was alone in the gym. What if it scared him so much he had a heart attack?

"But . . . nothing exploded," said Lena.

No. It hadn't. Not one single explosion.

Doubt flooded Maggie. *Did I do something wrong?* she whispered inside her head, questioning the only person who had the answer.

You've mixed that same formula before, said her father. *It's not that complicated, Maggie. Even Griggs could do it, and he's a complete tool.* Maggie heard a hint of disapproval in his voice, that impatience with people who make sloppy mistakes, who can't keep up.

The sound of voices approaching could be heard through the closed gym doors that led to the school hallway.

"We have to go!" said Lena. "Now!"

"We can't leave that flower in the middle of the basketball court!" protested Maggie. She could hear her father scolding. It was sloppy. Inelegant. Dangerous.

But Lena was already pulling on Maggie's arm. The two girls slipped out the secret door, jamming it closed behind them.

"It's too bad we won't get to see it happen," said Lena as they hurried around to the front of the school. The first students were beginning to stream down the hill.

"That's how it is with hacks," said Maggie. "You set them up, and then you disappear." *The private glory comes later when you know you did something no one else could even imagine.*

Maggie and Lena didn't have gym until Friday with Mrs. Dornbusch. It would be Mrs. Matlaw's class that had the honor of taking part in the Exploding Gym Class Hack. At least that was how it was supposed to work.

ELEVEN

BUT DURING HOMEROOM THAT MORNING, Mrs. Dornbusch made an unexpected announcement: she and Mrs. Matlaw were swapping gym days, and her class, which included Maggie and Lena, would meet in the gym next period. When Tyler asked why, Mrs. Dornbusch said, "I don't know and I don't care." She was deep into her crossword puzzle, and the word around school was that Mr. Platt had unwisely challenged her to a daily puzzle-off: whoever finished the crossword puzzle first each day won a bag of jelly beans from the loser. It was only the second day of school, but Mr. Platt had already had to provide a bag of Jelly Belly jelly beans, which Ms. Dornbusch was popping in her mouth as she worked the crossword.

"But Mrs. Dornbusch—" began Maggie.

Mrs. Dornbusch stared at her, a look of true

bafflement on her face. "Not Megan. Not Maria. Not Michelle . . ." Maggie opened her mouth to say, *My name is Maggie!* but the Gray Gargoyle waved her hand in the air as if to disperse a bad smell and said, "It doesn't matter." The bell rang. "March! With any luck, I can finish this puzzle while you all run laps."

There was nothing to do but walk to the gym. Mrs. Dornbusch made herself comfortable on a folding metal chair that was set up in the corner, and directed the children to jog around the edge. Riley was allowed to sit on a pile of wrestling mats due to his highly reactive airways.

Each time Maggie and Lena ran by, Mrs. Dornbusch would yell out a puzzle clue, such as, "What's an eight-letter word for 'Typewriters, for example'?" and by the time they had lapped the gym again, they would have the answer: "Obsolete!" Or "What's a nine-letter word for 'Not proven by fact' that ends in *e*?" That had taken two laps: "Debatable!"

"She's completely cheating," complained Maggie, who hated running laps more than any other activity on earth. It was so boring. "You're not allowed to get help in a puzzle-off."

Lena was practically walking, her long strides able to keep pace alongside Maggie with no trouble. "I'll bet you a bag of jelly beans I know what her answer would be if you told her that."

Without even a moment's pause, both girls answered, "I. Don't. Care!"

As they continued to run, Maggie and Lena were careful to keep well outside the lines of the basketball court. At one point, Max shoved Tyler so that Tyler took one step inside the lines, and Maggie would have gasped if she hadn't been so out of breath. But nothing happened. *It really is a dud*, she thought dispiritedly. But Lena nudged her and said, "Boy, is he lucky."

Lyle was the first to figure out that Mrs. Dornbusch didn't care whether they ran or not. He dropped out of the loop and settled on the ground with his back against the wall, content to spend the rest of gym taking a nap. In short order, the rest of the sixth graders stopped running as well. But Kayla felt that *someone* should take charge, and if it wasn't going to be Mrs. Dornbusch, it might as well be her.

"Let's do some stretching!" said Kayla enthusiastically. "It will be a good cooldown. I'll lead!"

Kayla walked—with that supreme confidence she always had—straight for the middle of the gym floor. Lena grabbed hold of Maggie's arm, and neither of them breathed as Kayla walked eight steps directly to the center of the gym.

"How did she *do* that?" whispered Lena ferociously. "Is she charmed or something?"

She's Kayla, Maggie thought, as if that explained everything. This was immediately followed by the thought, *I must have messed up*.

"What's that?" asked Colt, pointing to the daisy on the floor at the far end of the basketball court. Max, Tyler, Chris, and Stevie all advanced to investigate, just as Becky, Grace, Shana, Brianna, and Jenna approached Kayla to follow her lead in stretching.

Snap! There was a sound like a drum banging, and then a puff of gorgeous purple smoke rose up from Max's feet.

Crack! Another explosion of purple smoke ignited at Becky's feet, causing her to stumble backward, knocking over Brianna and Grace, who were close on her heels. The smoke looked like something from fairyland. A deep plum color and wispy, it dissipated within seconds, leaving nothing behind.

Pop! Pop! Chris jumped back, setting off two more little explosions, as three clouds of iris-violet smoke puffed into the air and then drifted away.

All the sixth graders immediately retreated to the edge of the gym.

"Cool!" shouted Max, pushing a foot forward to see if he could make another explosion go off.

"That scared me half to death!" said Becky, but she was laughing, now that the fright was over and she was safely on the sidelines.

"Somebody throw a shoe or something," said Max.

"Stop!" shouted Mrs. Dornbusch, who was on her feet, her crossword puzzle abandoned on the floor beside her.

Only Kayla was left stranded in the middle of the floor. She stared at her classmates, separated by the unstable ocean of the basketball court. Everyone else was safely ashore. She looked so . . . isolated. It was the first time Maggie could remember seeing a look of hesitation on Kayla's face. She was always so *sure*, so confident, but at this moment, she looked frightened.

Slowly, she backed up, away from the place where the other explosions had gone off.

Snap! Crack! Pop! Three puffs of purple smoke exploded, causing Kayla to hop from foot to foot. She turned wildly one way, then the other, desperately searching the floor for what was causing the blasts. But the floor was spotless, swept clean as it was every day by Mr. Fetterholf, who took such pride in his school, where he had been custodian for so many years.

Maggie watched. This was not how the hack was supposed to unfold. There was supposed to be joyful chaos, the whole class running rampant over the gym, the air filled with the snap, crackle, and pop of the harmless explosions and the beautiful, lilac-colored smoke. For Maggie, the hack would have been a triumph of science: the miraculous reaction of a compound and a cation. For Lena, it would have been an act of rebellion: an antidote to the iron fist of Principal Shute. Either way, it was meant to be fun.

But it was clear that Kayla *wasn't* having fun. And Maggie was *glad*. She knew she wasn't supposed to be. She knew that it was a terrible thing to take pleasure in someone else's pain, but deep inside of her, there was a part of Maggie that was happy that Kayla was miserable.

Serves her right, said her father. *Telling that story about you on the first day of school . . .*

Maggie agreed with her father. Kayla looked so scared, it occurred to her that maybe Kayla would wet her pants. *Ha! There's a story that no one would forget*, she thought. She imagined telling it at the lunch table. After all, turnabout was fair play. Right?

"Kayla!" said Mrs. Dornbusch sternly. "Listen to me! These explosions are harmless. They're nothing more than nitrogen triiodide. A party trick. Just run straight to me. Don't stop for anything. Just run." She held out her long, bony arms, as if she could shorten the distance between the two of them.

But Kayla was frozen. And who could blame her? Running *toward* the Gray Gargoyle? Most students in Odawahaka spent their years running away from the woman. Kayla couldn't move an inch from the spot where she stood. It was like she'd been turned to stone, except for a few solitary tears that leaked from her eyes. There was nothing anyone could do to help her.

And then the mouse parachuted from above. Lena had set it up when she had climbed to the rafters. A single rubber mouse, perched close enough to the edge so that the explosions would nudge it . . . just over.

It tumbled, falling head over heels, until its parachute opened, and it began to sail straight for Kayla's head, like a World War II paratrooper 'chuting into Normandy.

Kayla screamed, "A mouse!" and ran faster than Maggie could ever remember seeing a bipedal creature move. It was like Kayla had rocket boosters on her sneakers. Several explosions went off as she ran from the center of the basketball court to the edge, but she didn't stop.

As soon as the mouse landed, it set off the big show. Puffs of smoke erupted from the floor, and the air was filled with the percussive sounds of anarchy: explosions, cheers, whoops, and laughter.

When all was quiet again, Lyle turned to Mrs. Dornbusch and asked, "Can we run all over the court?"

Mrs. Dornbusch shrugged. "I don't care." She picked up her crossword puzzle and started to gnaw on her pencil.

All the boys raced for the mouse, but Max was the first to scoop it up. He held it aloft, showing the tiny sign the mouse carried in its paws: *ROAR!* As the students ran all over the court, searching for the last few remaining explosions, they tossed the mouse back and forth, shouting, "ROAR!" at the top of their lungs. Even Riley joined in the mayhem, wheezing slightly but not wanting to miss out on the fun. Only Kayla asked to be excused so that she could sit in the empty nurse's office and collect herself.

When the bell rang and the students finally filed out of the gymnasium—hot, sweaty, and bonded for life— Chris turned to Colt and said, "Best gym class ever." It was the first time he'd spoken directly to Colt since elementary school.

Colt nodded. "Like something in a book."

Lena nudged Maggie, a big smile on her face. But Maggie knew that Lena couldn't really understand the importance of these words. You had to have grown up in Odawahaka to see how things were changing.

TWELVE

"WELL, I THINK WE CAN BOTH agree that purple is not Kayla's color," said Lena as they walked to Lena's house.

"Not after today," agreed Maggie, laughing. "She'll never eat another plum again."

"Or an eggplant!"

"Yeah, but who would?" asked Maggie. "Eggplant is the grossest food known to humankind."

"I love eggplant!" argued Lena.

As they walked down 2½ Street, Maggie couldn't help thinking that Lena must feel a little embarrassed by the shabbiness, the complete and utter ruin of the houses in this particular part of town. Many of them were no more than rusted-out trailers set up on cinder blocks, with no electricity or even water hookups. Not that any section of Odawahaka was "fancy," but none was as depressing as this forgotten curl of a road that spiraled off from the right-angle streets like a pea shoot gone awry.

But Lena didn't seem embarrassed at all. "Ta-da! This is it!" she said, pointing to a house that sat at the top of a hill, almost entirely hidden by overgrown bushes. Yep. It was the house that everyone avoided on Halloween, abandoned for as long as Maggie could remember. A steep set of stairs made of cracked and crumbling concrete paraded in front of the girls. "Thirty-two steps," Lena said enthusiastically. "I like to take them two at a time." And she was off.

When they reached the rotting front porch, Maggie could see that the house was twice as large as hers, but half as solid. The porch banister had fallen off, the front windows were cracked, and the few remaining shutters were gap-toothed and hung crookedly.

"Watch it," said Lena, pointing to a hole in the floorboards near the threshold. Then she twisted the doorknob, jiggling it furiously, and kicked the door open. They both stepped inside.

The living room was empty except for a beautiful Oriental rug in the middle of the room, a single wooden chair, and a spindly antique table just large enough to hold a small vase of wildflowers. The floors were swept clean, and the window glass was spotless. Light flooded the room, pouring in through the tall, curtainless windows. There was a fresh coat of white paint on all the walls, as if they were expecting something worth displaying. Maggie had the feeling that she had stepped inside a bleached and abandoned seashell.

Lena led Maggie into the large kitchen, which was also drenched in sunlight. The stove looked like it might still run on coal and the refrigerator had rust spots. The green limestone sink had a divider down the middle: one half held glass jars filled with dirty paintbrushes and the other contained a pile of dishes left to soak. Lena opened the refrigerator and started to take inventory.

"What's this room?" Maggie looked around the corner from the kitchen into the largest room of all. In it, there was a tall easel and rows of canvases. There was one long table covered in painting supplies and another with all kinds of strange equipment: blocks of wood and long metal pipes and wooden paddles. Maggie's eyes locked on the table: she spotted five different kinds of acetylene blowtorches, along with safety gloves and goggles. Industrial grade! She worried she might begin to drool—specialized tools always made her heart beat fast. "What do your parents *do*?"

"Dad's a poet. Mom's an artist. She's in Paris right

now, helping set up a show for this really famous glass artist." Maggie picked up one of the torches. "He got Mom into it. That's what all that stuff is. He's got a one-man show at the Louvre. It's a big deal." Maggie wondered, Did she hear something that sounded like sadness in Lena's voice?

"Do you want ice cream or leftover lasagna?" asked Lena, her head buried in the refrigerator.

Maggie paused. "Both," she said.

"Well chosen, *sensei*," said Lena. She cut cubes of the cold lasagna and dished out bowls of blackberry ice cream. Maggie took a bite of the lasagna and was surprised by how good it tasted. It was obviously home-made, not something defrosted at the last minute.

After finishing her lasagna, Maggie carried her bowl of perfectly softened ice cream into the room with the glass-blowing equipment. Some of the tools looked positively medieval, but others were clearly high-tech. Maggie picked up a pair of spring-loaded calipers and pinched them on her nose so that they hung from her face. It looked like a strange nose-piercing that extended past her chin. She turned to Lena and said, "What do you think? My new look?" But her voice was so nasal it was hard to understand her words.

Lena laughed explosively, ice cream shooting out of

her mouth. "Very glam!" Then she picked up two pairs of heavy metal tongs and placed them on top of her head. "Mutant bunny ears!"

The two girls continued to move down the row of tools, repurposing them in bizarre and hilarious ways. When they reached the end of the row, Maggie scooped up the last puddle of her soupy ice cream and asked, "Where's your dad?"

"Out," said Lena. She moved back into the kitchen, where she put her empty bowl in the sink. "Wandering the countryside. Dad says poets who stay shut up in their own houses never have anything worth saying."

"Your parents are really different," said Maggie. "It would never occur to my mother to wander the countryside." Or go to Paris. Or anywhere, for that matter. "Your parents are *daring.*"

"I suppose . . . ," said Lena slowly. "They're artists. And artists are creative and nonconformists, but they're also sort of"—she wrinkled her nose, thinking of the right word—"self-absorbed. I mean, I don't blame them. You have to really *love* . . . your art." Lena's voice trailed off, and again there was the sound of sadness.

"I think all parents are kind of self-absorbed," said Maggie. "My mother spends half her time in her room when she's home." Maggie didn't mention the constant, low hum of the TV at night or the sound of ice clinking inside a refilled glass.

"Oh! I have something to show you!" Lena shouted, reaching out for Maggie's empty bowl and putting it in the sink alongside her own. "Something to *give* you. *Two* somethings, in fact. Come on!" Lena grabbed her camera, then hurried for the stairs. Maggie followed.

Lena's room, the last one at the end of the hall, was enormous. There were six floor-to-ceiling windows, all of them open, and a freestanding clothes rack that seemed to hold Lena's entire wardrobe, out for all to see. Right in the middle of the room, floating like an island, was a queen-sized bed with four posts made out of what looked like the trunks of white birch trees. Lashed to the posts were two old wooden ladders that formed a trellis across the top. Lena had woven long strips of silk cloth in every color over and through the ladders. The filmy ends hung down, forming a curtain on all four sides that fluttered and shifted with the faint breeze that came in through the open windows.

Maggie turned three hundred and sixty degrees around the room and stared at the walls. They were covered with enormous black-and-white photos of faces—or at least parts of faces. Two eyes, each six feet wide, looked down on the windows. A cheek. A nose. A perfect set of lips that seemed to be kissing the closet door. And on one wall there was an extreme close-up of a woman's smiling face.

"That's my mom," said Lena. "The day before she left."

"You put these up?" asked Maggie. "These are your photographs?" She continued to wander around the room as if it were an art museum, looking at images that were bizarre, frightening, beautiful, surprising. An eyelash as thick as her finger. A mole the size of her fist. Freckles that seemed to be a road map. An elbow that looked prehistoric. "How do you do this?" Maggie went up to the wall and ran her hands over the surface. The photos were pasted on, as perfectly as if the job had been done by a professional wallpaper hanger.

"In pieces," said Lena. "You can feel the places where they join. See. There. And there. So then I just piece them together to make the whole face. Or whatever part I want to focus on."

"Your parents let you do this?" Maggie thought about the time she'd asked to paint her room black so that she could conduct some light experiments. Grand-pop's answer had been, "Over your dead body."

"Why wouldn't they?" Lena seemed genuinely puzzled by the question.

Maggie had no response. Why *wouldn't* parents let

kids be kids? She couldn't take her eyes off the images. They were mesmerizing.

"Come on," said Lena.

Maggie had to literally hoist herself onto the bed, it was so high off the ground. "It's like being under a waterfall," she said, reaching out and running her fingers through the strands of colorful silk.

"I know," said Lena, rummaging through the books and papers, the laptop and discarded clothes that covered half the bed. "It's my favorite place in the whole house." Her hand dove under the rumpled covers and came up with a rolled-up poster tied with a frayed strip of orange silk fabric. "Here it is! For you!" She presented it like a scroll.

When Maggie unrolled the poster, it was a black-and-white photo from the 1930s of a woman holding a large box camera, perched on top of a skyscraper high above New York City.

"Margaret Bourke-White!" said Lena triumphantly. "One of the greatest American photographers who ever lived. And a woman. And a Margaret!"

"Wow," said Maggie. "How did you make this?"

"I have a large-format printer. For my work. I make posters all the time." Lena waved her hand at the walls of her room.

"What an epic place for a hack," said Maggie, staring at the image of the woman at the top of the building. "Imagine getting a police car up *there*. Thanks!" She trailed her fingertips along the surface of the poster, as if she could feel the building and the old box camera. "It's going straight up on my wall when I get home. It's the best Margaret of all."

"And now, present *deux!*" shouted Lena. She jumped off the bed and ran into a different room, then returned carrying a small color photograph. Her voice suddenly became serious. "For you."

Lena held out both hands, presenting the photograph to Maggie the way soldiers present a folded flag at the funeral of a fallen hero, with the utmost respect and gravity.

Maggie looked at the photograph. It was the same one she'd seen a thousand times, the one that was taped to her computer screen at home: her father standing on the lawn at MIT in front of the Great Dome. But in this photograph, Maggie was there, too. Right next to him. His arm was casually draped across her shoulder, and her arm was wrapped around his waist. They were staring at the camera and smiling. Both of them were smiling. Together at MIT.

"How did you . . . ?" Maggie reached forward, almost

afraid to touch it for fear it might dissolve. She took it from Lena, holding it in both hands, staring and staring at the image. She wanted to fall into the picture and never come out again.

"Do you like it?" asked Lena, her voice rising in excitement. "I am really, really good at Photoshop. I mean, insanely good. Like, I could join the CIA and do some crazy stuff. But I never would."

"It looks so real."

"But do you *like* it?" asked Lena, suddenly sounding worried, as if a thought that hadn't occurred to her before was suddenly worming its way into her brain.

Didn't see that coming, said Maggie's father's voice inside her head, clearly impressed.

"I love it more than anything else on earth." How had Lena known? How had she seen? Was it that obvious? The one thing she desired above all else? After all, she and Lena had met less than forty-eight hours ago. Scientifically, it didn't make sense.

Lena sighed happily. "You like it. I'm really glad." Then she dove under the covers again and rummaged until she resurfaced holding two Milky Way bars. She handed one to Maggie, who began to suspect that the bed was like a magician's hat. Who knew what Lena would pull from it next?

Lena ripped open the wrapper of her candy bar and took a giant bite. "You know," she said, her words mangled by the goo of caramel on her teeth, "I've been thinking about our next hack. . . ."

THIRTEEN

"THE MOUSE IS IN THE HOUSE! The Mouse is in the house!" became a frequent chant at Oda M in the next few weeks.

At Table 10, arguments erupted on a daily basis about where each new hack ranked on the Top Ten list of Mouse attacks.

Jenna declared, "Absolutely number one: when Principal Shute's entire desk was wrapped in 'mouse-king' tape. Did you see it? The desk looked like a mummy, and there was a little toy mouse wearing a crown sitting on top of it. It was the cutest thing ever!"

"No," said Tyler, shaking his head vigorously. "The best one was when Principal Shute was doing the morning announcements and he kept getting interrupted by the sound of squeaking. Every time he started a sentence . . . SQUEAK! I mean, when was the last time you heard a principal swear during morning announcements?"

"Actually," said Lyle, "my favorite was the day we came to the cafeteria and there were spray cans of Easy Cheese at each table. What's better than liquid cheese you can spray right into your mouth? Nothing!"

"Yeah, except Tyler sprayed it up my nose!" said Max.

"Your fault," said Tyler. "You moved."

The Mouse is in the house! The Mouse is in the house!

The third Monday, the students noticed something peculiar on the front door of the school. It was a traffic sign that looked so real, you would have thought it was stolen from one of the signposts in town, except that there was one little difference:

WARNING: MOUSE WORK AHEAD

PROCEED AT YOUR OWN RISK

Throughout the school, signs were posted on doors, on walls, on railings and desks. They looked like real road signs, down to every detail.

NO PARKING: MOUSE LANE

STATE LAW: YIELD TO MOUSE

PUSH BUTTON FOR MOUSEWALK

WEIGHT LIMIT 10 MICE

Principal Shute was in a fury—and was doing a poor job of hiding the fact. All day long, the students could see him tearing down the signs as quickly as he discovered them, but new signs kept appearing. These were hastily drawn, each one in different handwriting, scribbled on blank sheets of notebook paper or on the back sides of class handouts:

NO STOPPING: MOUSE LOADING ZONE

MAX HEIGHT: 50 MICE

TURN BACK: WRONG MOUSE

No matter how vigilantly Mr. Shute patrolled the halls, the signs kept popping up. By lunchtime, someone had taped a cartoon on the door to the empty, locked library; it showed a man wielding a baseball bat, with the caption: *Principal Shute plays Whack-a-Mouse.*

The Mouse is in the house! The Mouse is in the house!

You could hear it chanted in the cafeteria, in the

classrooms, in the rotunda, even at football games, where the Wildcats were off to an incredible start to the season, having beaten the Mifflinburg Miners 40–14, the Bloomsburg Huskies 47–0, the Central Columbia Blue Jays 42–21, and the Warrior Run Defenders 57–0.

This week, the entire town was gearing up for Friday night's away game with the Lewisburg Panthers, but on Thursday night, Lena and Maggie found themselves creeping through the darkened halls of Oda M on their way to the cafeteria. Both girls carried heavy backpacks and were dressed all in black. Maggie was wearing a dark purple Wildcats ski cap. She had stuffed as much of her wildly unmanageable hair under it as she could, but a few stray strands of yellow curls exploded about her face.

"How do you even know about this secret passageway?" asked Lena. They were making their way to the balcony that overlooked the cafeteria.

"It's not a secret passageway," said Maggie. "It's more of a utility corridor."

"It's hidden and it's locked. That makes it a secret passageway in my book."

"This is it," said Maggie. The hallway became the top level of the cafeteria here, forming a balcony that looked down on the main dining room, originally built to hold five hundred students at once. It seemed strange to think that there'd been a time in Odawahaka when such a school was necessary: a sprawling school, a growing school, a school full of energy and potential and ambition. Even in the darkness, Maggie could feel the bigness of it—the empty, unused space all around them. She and Lena were like two marbles rolling around in a large, empty shoe box.

"Flip on your headlamp," said Maggie as she switched hers on.

Both girls wore camping lights strapped to their foreheads, and Maggie pulled a bobby pin from the hair at the base of her neck. (She always kept a few stashed there, just in case.) She snapped the bobby pin in two, bent one half to create a tension wrench, and bit off the plastic nub on the other half to create the pick. She knelt down in front of what appeared to be a small cupboard door, wiggled both pieces of the bobby pin into the lock, and had it sprung in less than fifteen seconds.

"Very James Bond!" whispered Lena.

"No," said Maggie sadly. "It's a crummy lock. I could have picked it with my teeth." Sometimes, she wished the school presented more of a challenge. It made her feel less than her father to have such easy obstacles to overcome.

Your time will come, whispered her father.

"Okay, in we go," said Maggie. She crawled on her hands and knees into the small passageway. It was like a square miner's tunnel, three feet wide by three feet high.

"Whoa!" said Lena. "I thought you said it was a hallway."

"Think of it as a small hallway. A hallway for . . ." She was about to say *mice*, but then stopped herself. Probably not the best way to get Lena to enter. *We really have become the mice in the walls of Oda M!*

"I didn't think it would be that small." Lena backed away. "I thought we'd be able to stand up, or at least stoop."

"It's plenty big," said Maggie. "See? It's easy to turn around." She showed Lena how simple it was to maneuver in the tight space. Of course, she was much smaller than Lena and had always liked the feeling of being in close quarters. When she was little, she used to crawl inside the clothes dryer just to relax.

Lena kept backing away. "We've only known each other for about four weeks, so I might not have mentioned this yet, but I'm crazy-mad claustrophobic. I think it's why I enlarge my photos. I like things *big*. Big art. Big food. Big rooms. Big beds." The whole time she was talking, she was slowly backing away.

"Lena," said Maggie. "You can do this."

"I can't even step into a closet!" said Lena. "Did you notice in my room? All my clothes hang on racks."

"I thought it was just some kind of artist thing," said

Maggie, flashing her headlamp on Lena's face.

"No, it's because I have out-of-control panic attacks. I can't do small spaces."

Maggie started to laugh. She couldn't help it. *She* was afraid of heights, and *Lena* was afraid of small spaces. What a hacking team they made!

The incapacitated leading the incapable, muttered her father.

"Hey!" said Maggie. She thought that comment was uncalled for. After all, one way or another, they'd managed to pull off each hack.

"Hey, what?" asked Lena.

"Hey . . . I need you," said Maggie. "It takes two people to work the pulley system, and I can't take down the interior panel by myself. You *have* to come in here."

"I don't know that I can," said Lena. Her voice sounded very small. *We really have turned into mice,* thought Maggie.

You are not *mice,* said her father. *You are colossal. Monumental. Unstoppable.*

"Try this," said Maggie. "Take out your camera and look through the lens. Tunnel vision, same as when you take photos. Just keep looking through your camera. The whole world around you doesn't exist. Just what you see through the lens. Then work your way forward, slowly, looking through your camera."

As Maggie spoke, Lena entered the tunnel, her camera held in front of her eye.

"Good!" said Maggie. "Just keep inching forward. You're doing great! Now see these latches?" she asked. "There are four of them. You need to undo each latch, while I hold onto these knobs, or else the whole panel will crash to the ground." Lena continued holding the camera lens to her eye with one hand as her other hand fiddled with the latches. Maggie removed the panel, and suddenly they were staring out over the cafeteria from thirty feet up in the air.

"Okay, now I'm fine," said Lena, putting her camera down. "As long as I'm not closed in, I'm totally okay."

Maggie swooned backward. "I might throw up." She turned away from the thirty-foot drop and stared at the closed dark space of the passageway, which made her feel safe. Enclosed. "How does that make any sense that you feel okay now?" she asked. "It's not like you could jump out of the hole if you had to! The fall would kill you!"

Lena reached for her backpack. "Well, it's not like you're suddenly going to catapult over the edge. Phobias don't make sense. They're irrational. What do we do next?"

Maggie examined the pulley system that held the football banners in place and felt her spirits sag. It was exactly as she had feared: the pulleys were so rusty that the links in each chain had practically fused together from neglect. Not only that, but actual mice had built nests in the gears, jamming up the mechanism. They had gnawed most of the way through one of the cables that attached to the fifty-pound counterweight, and they had chewed extensively on the wooden shaft that anchored the pins in place.

"You know," said Maggie as she retrieved a can of oil from her backpack and began to grease the chain, "mice are small, but when they work together, they can do impressive things."

They unhooked the old banners from the pulley system and allowed them to flutter to the cafeteria floor below. Then Lena pulled the "new" banners from her backpack and hung them according to Maggie's instructions.

When Maggie and Lena (both happy to be out of the tunnel and back on the ground) inspected their work from below, they had to admit, it was hard to notice that anything had changed.

"The perfect hack," said Maggie.

No hack is perfect, her father reminded her, but Maggie decided to ignore that particular comment.

"How long can it possibly take one human being to *look up?*" asked Lena. For the past twenty-five minutes, not one student in the cafeteria had noticed the new banners. All anyone was talking about was that night's game against the Lewisburg Panthers—one of the toughest teams the Wildcats would face all season. Lunch period was nearly over, and no one had noticed that the banners were different. Lena had worked *hard* on those banners, and Maggie knew she was impatient for the fun to begin.

But Maggie smiled knowingly. "Sometimes you have to wait. Each hack unfolds in its own time, in its own way."

"You sound like a Zen master," complained Lena.

No, I sound like my dad, Maggie thought. "Don't worry," she said, putting a hand on Lena's shoulder. "There's always something that comes along, shakes things loose, gets the ball rolling. . . ."

"Listen up!"

The sixth graders stopped their chattering and turned as one to look at the balcony where Principal Shute stood, directly over the clock. The banners hung in front of him, one on each side. "I have an announcement to make. It concerns the use of paper towels in the boys' bathrooms!"

Mr. Shute began a long harangue about the problem of wadded-up paper towels and overflowing sinks, as seventy-one sixth graders stared up at their principal—and the banners that flanked him.

Lena punched Maggie in the arm.

"Wait for it," said Maggie. "Wait for it. . . ."

Colt was the first to notice, probably because his eyes were so well trained to read any words put in front of them. "Who changed the banners?" he asked.

"Yeah," said Shana. "The words are different."

"And that's a *mouse*," said Brianna. "Or a very fat woodchuck."

"It's a mouse!" shouted Lena, and the decibel level in the cafeteria began to rise as more and more students noticed the altered banners.

The first banner looked exactly as it always had, except that the roaring Wildcat had been replaced with a smiling mouse whose ridiculously long tail oscillated along the edge of the sign. The slogan on the banner read, *There is no substitute for WAVELENGTH and no excuse for a CRACK IN IT.*

The second banner showed a chubby mouse staring over its enormous, round belly with the words: *The WHISKERS and TAIL of the Odawahaka Wildmouse will not be entrusted to the WICKED or the SQUEAK.*

Principal Shute continued to talk, threatening severe disciplinary measures if the use of paper towels was not immediately brought under control, but the unmistakable chant had begun: "The Mouse is in the house! The Mouse is in the house!" It grew louder and louder.

"I told you," whispered Maggie. "*Something* always comes along that gets the ball rolling. You just never know what it's going to be."

"Shute!" whispered Lena gleefully.

"What is going on down there?" demanded the principal, descending the staircase and turning to see what the students were staring at.

He read the banners, several times. They looked *so close* to right. But they were very, very wrong. "Take them down!" he shouted, pointing at the offending signs. "Immediately. Get a ladder. Get two ladders. I want those banners off the walls. Now!"

Mr. Fetterholf, who was always on hand during lunch, readjusted the Wildcats baseball cap on his head. "Well," he said, "I'm not sure a ladder will do the trick. That's not how the banners were hung forty years ago, and that's not how these ones are coming down today."

"What do you mean?" A large blood vessel on Principal Shute's neck bulged over his tight collar. Maggie couldn't help wondering if it was going to explode. She was surprised at how infuriated the principal was. After all, it wasn't as if the banners were a danger. They weren't about to fall and crush anyone. They weren't about to reach out and strangle a passing student. What was so important about getting them down *immediately*?

"What is his problem?" asked Lena, leaning over to Maggie.

"It's disrespectful!" said Kayla indignantly. She crossed her arms, personally offended by the banners and their cheerful smiling mice.

Mr. Fetterholf was patiently explaining to the principal, "There's a pulley system. Behind the wall. There's a passageway that gives us access to the clock and the lights and the pulleys. Now, look over there. You see that panel? You'd have to be *inside* the passageway to take it down. So whoever hung those banners was inside the passageway. And frankly, I don't know who could have done *that*." He looked around at the sixth graders and smiled. "Except the mice!" Even when Mr. Fetterholf had been a student, there had been legends about the manic mice at Oda M.

"Well, get inside the passageway and take those banners down!"

Mr. Fetterholf scratched his chin thoughtfully. "Sure, I can do it. But it's going to take some time. I can't remember for the life of me where the key is for that door. And you have to be careful. You don't want that panel falling thirty feet onto someone's head. Right?" He looked over at Colt DuPrey and smiled, his eyes sparkling.

"Those banners are coming down *this instant*," shouted Principal Shute. He called out to several of the boys, scattering students as he advanced. "Push the table up against the wall," he directed. "You two, that side. You, on this side with me." He was clearly a man who was used to giving orders.

"Mr. Shute," said Mrs. Matlaw cautiously, "I don't think anything of this sort should be undertaken with the students in the cafeteria."

"Why not?" said Mr. Shute. "Let them see what happens when vandalism takes place at our school. This type of rogue behavior will be stamped out, Mrs. Matlaw. *Stamped out.* I will not have a lack of discipline swallow up the proud traditions of this school. Not on my watch!"

He vaulted onto the tabletop, pulled up a chair, and then climbed on top of it.

Maggie and Lena both knew how securely the banners were attached to the pulley system. And the system had been designed to withstand decades of strain.

With both hands, Mr. Shute reached over his head, grasped the lower edge of the first banner, and yanked on the fabric. It wouldn't give. The metal chains of the pulley system were too strong. He pulled again. Maggie could see the dark circles of sweat under his arms and the vein on his neck swell. But the banner stayed in place. Finally, with a grunt of effort, he jumped off the chair. There was a tremendous sound of ripping fabric and the clatter of his feet landing on the hard tabletop. Lena sucked in her breath. She had spent nearly twenty hours making that banner and Principal Shute had destroyed it in less than thirty seconds. He quickly bundle-wrapped the tangle of fabric and handed it to Mrs. Matlaw, who looked grieved to be receiving it, as if it was a body.

Mr. Shute jumped to the ground. He threw his weight against the table, exhorting, "Move it. Slide it along." The next minute he was back on top of the table, climbing up the chair and reaching for the bottom edge of the second banner. Because of the location of a water fountain just underneath the banner, it was harder to press the table up against the wall, so it was more difficult for Mr. Shute to reach the second banner. By stretching far over his head, he just managed to gather up a handful of the soft, slippery satin. He tugged, but the fabric held. He reached with his other hand and just managed to catch the bottom corner of the banner. He pulled, nearly lifting himself off the chair. Maggie felt Lena's hand grasp her upper arm, squeezing tightly.

"This is not going to end well," intoned Lyle.

It was inevitable, Maggie realized. The reaching, the pulling, the instability of the table, as well as the general unreliability of sixth-grade boys who can't resist the opportunity to pull chairs out from under people. Before anyone could figure out what had really happened, Principal Shute was hanging by the banner, his face pressed against the wall, his two legs desperately churning underneath him, trying to find the chair, which had fallen over.

But Lena had done her work and done it well. The banner held. It held, and it held.

And then it didn't.

With the same ripping sound that had accompanied the triumphant removal of the first banner, the second one came down. And with it came Principal Shute, landing on the water fountain and soaking a particularly embarrassing spot on his pants. He clumsily dropped to the floor, the silky banner fluttering on top of his head.

At the same time, the rigging that had held the banner in place dislodged a blue paper airplane, which came floating down to the outstretched hands of the sixth graders. Lyle was in the right spot (and the tallest) to reach up and grab it. He opened it and quickly read the words on the page.

FOURTEEN

"WHAT DOES IT SAY?" ASKED BECKY, crowding close.

"I should be the one to read it," said Kayla, stepping forward. "I *am* the class president!"

Maggie noticed that Jenna and Colt had both gathered behind Lyle, trying to catch a glimpse of the note, too.

"The banners are safe!" announced Lyle.

"Give that to me!" shouted Mr. Shute, snatching the note out of Lyle's hand and reading it quickly. He pointed at Kayla. "You come with me." Then he turned to the assembled sixth grade and shouted, "Lunch is dismissed! File out! That's an *order!*" He stormed out of the cafeteria followed by Kayla, who was pleased once again to be chosen above all the others.

After a moment of stunned silence, the other sixth

graders returned to their lunch tables to dispose of their trash and walked back to their classrooms.

The students assigned to Table 10 were the last to leave. Jenna turned to Lyle and asked, "What was on the piece of paper?" Maggie had hardly ever heard Jenna speak and she was surprised to hear a hint of determination behind her quiet words. Colt, Maggie, and Lena gathered closer to hear his answer.

"It's a scavenger hunt!" said Lyle. "A scavenger hunt that leads to the hiding place of the original banners. And that piece of paper was the first clue."

"What was the clue?" asked Colt. He was still holding the action adventure book he was reading, but he had closed it, marking his page with a bookmark.

Lyle closed his eyes. He took a deep breath in, then exhaled slowly.

> *Hydrogen, lithium,*
> *Sodium, barium.*
> *The airplane's a must.*
> *Beware. Don't combust.*

"How did you remember that?" asked Maggie. She'd *written* the poem, and even she couldn't recite it.

"I have amazing mental faculties," said Lyle, his eyes

regaining their usual sleepy appearance. "You'd never guess it, would you?"

"Not in a million years," said Colt.

Jenna meanwhile had scribbled down the clue on a piece of paper. She showed it to the others, circling the first two lines. "Chemistry."

Colt pointed to the word *airplane*. "B-1 Bomber."

And Lyle repeated, "Combust." He smiled. "My favorite: Bunsen burners."

The bell rang. Lunch was officially over. The sixth graders had to go to their next classes. In two minutes, they would be marked late.

"I've got science next," said Jenna.

"I'll escort you!" said Lyle.

"And we'll escort Lyle," said Colt. "Because—he really can't be trusted on his own."

"Too true," agreed Lyle, solemnly nodding his head. "Too true."

Jenna, Lyle, Colt, Maggie, and Lena raced downstairs, bursting into Mrs. Dornbusch's classroom just before the late bell.

FIFTEEN

"WHAT ARE YOU DOING?" THE B-1 Bomber demanded of Colt, Jenna, Lyle, Maggie, and Lena, who were spreading like ants across the classroom and disappearing behind the lab tables. "And why are you opening my supply cupboards?"

"We're looking for mice!" said Lyle. "We heard they're coming out of the walls and might be in your cupboards."

Mrs. Dornbusch strode forward, nostrils flaring, fists at her sides. "They wouldn't *dare*," she said.

"Found it!" said Colt, popping up from behind a lab table. In his hand, he held a piece of blue paper rolled into a scroll, which he had just plucked from the neck of an Erlenmeyer flask.

"Well, thank you!" boomed a voice from across the room. It was Principal Shute, followed closely by Kayla, who had clearly helped him unravel the clue. Principal Shute crossed the room and snatched the paper from Colt.

The Gray Gargoyle looked stonily at the principal. It was clear she'd rather have a herd of flatulent elephants in her classroom than him, but Maggie could see she wasn't about to come to the rescue of the sixth graders—especially when she didn't know precisely what was going on.

"Jenna, in your seat," she said. "The rest of you—out." It was unclear whether she meant *only* Lyle, Colt, Maggie, and Lena—or Principal Shute, too. In any case, Mr. Shute left first, and Maggie could see him hurrying off in the direction of the school's trophy case—the hiding place of the next clue in the scavenger hunt.

"Mrs. Dornbusch?" asked Maggie urgently. "Could we please have late passes? The bell's about to ring."

Mrs. Dornbusch waved impatiently at them. "I don't care," she grumbled, and tore four blank late passes off the pad in her desk. "Fill them out yourselves."

Once out in the hall, Lena looked sharply at Maggie, who gave her a *what do you want me to do?* look in return. This hack was not turning out as they had planned, at all.

Lena turned to the others. "It doesn't seem in the spirit of the thing, does it? A scavenger hunt is supposed to be fun. And everyone is supposed to join in."

"Not in Principal Shute's Army," said Lyle glumly. They were climbing the stairs to the main floor, heading to their next classes.

"Marines," corrected Colt. *"Semper fidelis.* Always loyal," he said.

"The worst part is that it isn't even a fair fight, because he stole the clue from us," said Lyle just as he reached the top of the flight of stairs. "We don't even know what it said. And *we* found it!"

At that moment Maggie tripped on the top step. She started to stumble forward, but before she could catch herself, Lyle reached out to grab her. Unfortunately, instead of helping to hold her steady, he accidentally shoved her backward. As she fell, she saw Lyle's face expand in terror: his eyes grow wider, his forehead stretch, his mouth open in a giant O. She was so surprised by what his face looked like (fully inflated!) that she hardly realized she was falling down an entire flight of stairs.

Until she landed.

"Oh my gosh, Maggie!" shouted Lena, racing down the steps. "Are you okay? You're bleeding!" She leaned over and used her T-shirt, which happened to be the Dada one, to wipe at Maggie's lip.

Well, that's appropriate, said her father. *Anarchy leads to bloodshed.*

Colt stripped off his hoodie and handed it to Lena. "In case she goes into shock."

"I am not going into shock," said Maggie. She was embarrassed by her own clumsiness, and more than a little frightened and stunned by the amount of blood running from her mouth.

Lyle shoved his hand in her face. "How many fingers do you see?"

"Four," answered Maggie, pulling herself to a sitting position and gently probing her lip. It was definitely swelling up. But she ran her tongue over her teeth and was relieved to feel that they were all where they were supposed to be.

"Wrong," said Lyle. "I'm holding up five fingers." He turned to Lena. "Is that a sign of a concussion?"

"Four fingers!" insisted Maggie. "The thumb is *not* a finger. It's a digit."

"She's fine," said Colt flatly. "*And* she's right about the thumb." But when they helped her up, she couldn't put weight on her right foot because she'd twisted the ankle.

"I'll run ahead to Mrs. McDermott and tell her she needs to telephone the nurse on call," said Colt. Maggie couldn't help but notice that Colt was pretty good in a crisis.

Lyle and Lena offered to form a chair with their arms and carry her, but the thought alarmed Maggie so much that she insisted she could walk on her own. And really, by the time they got to the office, she was feeling okay. Her ankle was a little banged up, but she could walk on it. She just wanted to rinse her mouth out with some salt water and stick a Band-Aid on her left knee. But Mrs. McDermott made her sit on the sick bed while she went back to the main office to call the nurse. There was no way of knowing how long it would take her to arrive. She covered five towns.

Colt read his book while Lyle leaned against the wall. Lena wandered the room, taking photographs of the nurse's office. There was a glass apothecary jar filled with cotton balls on the nurse's table.

"Have you ever noticed," said Lena, "that cotton balls look like marshmallows?"

Maggie and Lena exchanged a look. Colt continued to read his book, but Lyle straightened up to get a better view of the jar.

"I think they look like cotton candy," said Maggie.

"Or meringue!" said Lena.

"Or those sugary candy eggs at Easter."

"Or delicious scoops of vanilla ice cream!"

Lyle ambled over to the jar and reached a hand out for one of the cotton balls. He slowly pulled it apart and delicately sniffed it.

Unbelievable! whispered Maggie's father. *He's actually going to eat it!*

But before Lyle could pop the cotton ball in his mouth, he caught sight of something underneath the glass jar. It was a piece of blue paper exactly like the one that had fluttered out of the banner in the cafeteria. Lyle unfolded it.

"Unbelievable," he said, as though echoing Maggie's father. "It's the final clue in the scavenger hunt. The *last clue.*"

Colt hurried over. Maggie jumped up from the sick bed, wincing slightly as she put weight on her twisted ankle. Lena followed close behind, ready to catch her friend in case she fell.

"What are the chances?" asked Colt.

"It's *fate!*" said Lena. "Destiny. We were meant to find the football banners. Not Principal Shute and Kayla."

"Read it!" said Maggie to Lyle. "Mr. Shute has the other clues and Kayla is helping him, which means they're headed *here.* They could walk in at any moment!"

Lyle read the words in his slow, unhurried voice.

THE FINAL CLUE

Sometimes feel like you're the new kid in town?
Nobody gets you, thinks you're a clown?
Like a mammal that lays an egg, you don't fit,
"And" in Spanish, stuck in the middle of it.

Lena, Maggie, Lyle, and Colt all looked at one another.

"Huh?" said Colt.

"Like a Dada poem," said Lena wryly, looking at Maggie with great meaning.

"Well, even Dada poems have a purpose," Maggie responded, a little defensively. "*If* you can figure them out."

"But that's the problem, isn't it?" said Lena. Maggie and Lena had argued last night for nearly an hour about that final clue. Lena was sure that no one would be able to decipher it.

"Is it about you?" asked Lyle, looking at Lena. "You're the only new kid in town."

"It doesn't matter!" said Maggie. The bleeding from her lip had stopped. She grabbed a few Band-Aids to cover up her scraped knee. "We have to get out of here. As long as we have the last clue . . ."

Colt pushed open the door that led to the hallway but backed up so quickly, he stepped on Maggie, who let out a small shriek of pain.

"He's coming. Straight this way." Colt didn't have to say who *he* was.

Wow, thought Maggie. *Kayla is fast.*

Lyle still held the piece of blue paper in his hand. "What should we do?" Lena asked, frantically looking around the room. "Should we hide it under the mattress? Or throw it in the trash?"

"He'll find it, no matter where you put it," said Maggie. "He'll tear the room apart looking for it." She understood people like Mr. Shute. Sometimes, *she* was like Mr. Shute.

"Now would be a good time to have a Bunsen burner," said Lyle philosophically.

"Can't you memorize it?" asked Colt impatiently.

Lyle looked at the paper. "I can't memorize something that doesn't make any sense. Not in five seconds."

"We need to *do* something!" said Lena. She grabbed the paper out of Lyle's hand and quickly snapped a close-up of the note with her camera. Then she waved the paper, as if it were a grenade that was about to explode. "How can we get rid of this?"

Lyle grabbed the piece of paper out of her hand and

quickly tore it into tiny pieces. Then he shoved the scraps into his mouth, chewed five or six times, and swallowed. Lena and Maggie stared at him as if he had just eaten a live squid.

"That was truly awesome," said Colt in a hushed voice.

The door opened. Mr. Shute barreled in, then pulled up short. "What are *you* doing here?"

Lena pointed at Maggie's swollen lip. Lyle burped.

"I'm okay," said Maggie. "I've got these." She held up the Band-Aids in her hand.

"We better go," said Lena. "We don't want to miss any more social studies. We're studying the Mayans. They invented chocolate. I love chocolate." She inched toward the door and was the first to pass Mr. Shute. Then came Colt, followed closely by Maggie, who was limping just slightly. Lyle brought up the rear.

"Wait!" said Mr. Shute. "What is that?"

Lyle poked his head back into the room as Mr. Shute bent down and picked up a single scrap of blue paper the size of a postage stamp.

There was a long moment of silence. Maggie held her breath.

"Trash?" said Lyle, shrugging, and they all walked out.

SIXTEEN

HIDDEN IN THE STAIRWELL, LENA PULLED up the photo on her camera screen and read the clue aloud.

> *Sometimes feel like you're the new kid in town?*
> *Nobody gets you, thinks you're a clown?*
> *Like a mammal that lays an egg, you don't fit,*
> *"And" in Spanish, stuck in the middle of it.*

"What's that animal that's like a beaver with a big nose?" asked Lyle. "It starts with a *p*."

Oh, Lyle, thought Maggie, or maybe it was her father whispering the words inside her head.

"Platypus!" Colt said. "A platypus is the only mammal that lays eggs."

"Actually, no. Echidnas lay eggs, too," said Maggie.

"Maggie!" said Lena, turning to look at her severely. "No one's ever heard of that animal."

"Well, you still can't rule it *out*," said Maggie. If there was one thing she'd learned from her father it was the danger of skipping over possible solutions just because they seem unlikely.

"*Yes*," said Lena meaningfully. "But that isn't particularly helpful *at this moment*." She turned back to Colt. "I'm sure you're right. The clue must have something to do with a platypus. The only *well-known* mammal that lays eggs."

Lyle and Colt were quiet, each thinking in his own way. Finally Lyle spoke. "The Spanish word for 'and' is *y*." Lena, Maggie, and Colt all took French with Mr. Esposito, but Lyle studied Spanish.

Oh, thank you, Maggie said inside her head. When she and Lena had imagined the scavenger hunt, they had thought the whole school would take part, teaming up to compete, which was why the last clue had to be challenging. She had never imagined it would come down to Lyle Whittaker and Colt DuPrey figuring it out *all by themselves*. Or else losing to Principal Shute.

Lyle looked at the camera screen again. "Plat-y-pus," he said slowly. "Plat *and* pus." He looked stumped.

"Wait," said Colt. "*Platt* and *puss*." A huge grin spread

across his face. "Detour! Math class!"

As Colt and Lyle hurried ahead, Maggie whispered to Lena, "I thought they'd never get it."

Lena whispered back, "Did you really mean to fall down the stairs?"

"No! I was just going to pretend to bang my shin. But Lyle got in the way!"

Lena wrapped an arm around Maggie's shoulder. "Talk about taking one for the team! You're an inspiration, Maggie Gallagher."

"Well, how else were we going to get to the nurse's office? I mean, come on! *Five* fingers!" she scoffed. Then she realized that she sounded like her father, criticizing others for not being as quick as he was.

"Lyle did fine," said Lena. "Not to mention eating the evidence."

"Okay. That was supercool."

The bell rang and students poured into the hall. Maggie, Lena, Colt, and Lyle pushed their way into Room 217, swimming against the tide. "Hey, Mr. Platt!" said Lyle. "Can I take a look at the lion? The big one on top of your filing cabinet?"

Mr. Platt smiled, delighted to see them. "I thought you might be here to ask about the Robotics Club meeting next week! Any interest? Any interest at all?"

"No, sir. Just want to look at the big kitty cat!" Lyle reached for the stuffed toy and flipped it over. On the underside was a neatly sewn zipper that ran the length of the lion's belly.

"Why, I don't remember there being a zipper," said Mr. Platt, perplexed.

Lyle unzipped the lion and found the original banners inside. They had been washed and ironed. A separate note for Mr. Fetterholf explained that the pulley system was in top condition—cleaned, oiled, and realigned—so that it would now work without *squeaking*. (The Eighth Commandment of the Hacker's Bible: *Leave detailed instructions for how to disassemble a hack safely, and leave a site in better shape than you found it.*)

As Maggie headed for the door in Mr. Platt's room, she noticed the upper left corner of his blackboard. Every day, Mr. Platt wrote something—a famous quotation or a piece of advice or just a weird fact—in that spot. He called it his Daily Platt-itude.

Today's Daily Platt-itude was one of Maggie's father's favorite quotations. It was by a British computer scientist named Tony Hoare:

INSIDE EVERY LARGE PROBLEM IS A SMALL PROBLEM STRUGGLING TO GET OUT.

Maggie smiled. It made her feel that her father was *there*, in the room with her, and proud of her hack.

Mr. Fetterholf quietly replaced the banners after the students had gone home for the day. But it had not gone unnoticed by the sixth-grade class that even though Principal Shute had given a direct order to return to their classrooms, five of their classmates had set out on a quest to regain the missing banners. And those five students had prevailed.

Of course, it hadn't gone unnoticed by Principal Shute, either.

SEVENTEEN

THAT NIGHT'S GAME IN LEWISBURG WAS a huge victory. The Wildcats beat the Panthers 31–14, with the leading score
changing sides several times during the game. The fans
rolled into the town square on the victory buses, waving
noisemakers, reliving the highlights of the game, and
celebrating their no-name team and the unstoppable
force of their players, who had won the first five games
of the season.

But they never expected to see what awaited them
when the buses parked in front of the Opera House. The
H in *House* had been mysteriously transformed into an
M, and there was a six-foot papier-mâché mouse on the
roof of the three-story building, singing Mozart's *The
Marriage of Figaro*. Ringing the streets in front of the
Opera House were paper lanterns in every color, glowing

with a soft light that made the town look magical.

"It's the Opera Mouse!" shouted Max and Tyler, jumping off the bus and immediately running up to the old building and peering through the darkened windows. When they realized that the front door of the abandoned building was open and the entryway was filled with cases and cases of bottled Moxie—with a sign that said, *Enjoy a Moxie, on the Mouse!*—the gathering became a block party and victory celebration all in one.

The thrill of winning the first five games of the season, along with pride at hearing opera pouring out of the broken-down Opera House, seemed to awaken something in the townspeople. Neighbors stayed and talked, chatting about the game, catching up on news, enjoying the music, and even breaking into spontaneous dance. From time to time, the chant of "The Mouse is in the house! The Mouse is in the house!" would rise up from the crowd, and it was no longer just the sixth graders who were calling out the words. No one could recall the last time the town had gathered to celebrate like this.

"It was worth it," said Lena, throwing an arm over Maggie's shoulder and lifting her bottle of Moxie in salute. By "it," she meant the hours spent building the mouse and the near-death experience of hoisting all the equipment onto the roof of the Opera House.

Maggie shook her head. "You're the one who climbed hand over hand up the fire escape," she said, looking at the treacherous, hundred-year-old metal staircase that crawled up the side of the Opera House. "I just about died when you slipped at the third floor!" Without Lena, the hack would have been impossible. She had even hung a row of football-shaped piñatas underneath the mouse on a long wire that stretched from one end of the Opera House to the other.

"But I made it," said Lena. "Freaky strong arms!" And she raised both arms over her head in a sign of victory. "Besides, you're the one who squeezed into the tiny space under the floorboards for the wiring. *And* who rigged up the speakers and the spotlights and the beautiful fairy lanterns." Lena twirled around, spilling her Moxie on Maggie in the process.

"Yuck!" said Maggie, rubbing at the dampened sleeves of her coat. "This stuff is *sticky.*"

"That's the thing about Moxie," said Lena, taking a big swig. "You either love it or you hate it. And I love it! All of it!" And she twirled again, because the night was magical, and who knew what could happen next.

Maggie did. Without telling Lena, she had wired the piñatas with micro-detonators. The football-shaped decorations hung in a row along the top edge of the Opera

House, just below where the giant mouse sang in Italian. As the opera reached its crescendo, Maggie pushed the small remote control in her hand.

One by one, the piñatas burst open, their contents cascading to the delighted crowd below: confetti and candy and whistles and noisemakers and tiny pennant flags that read, *Go, Wildcats!* on one side and *ROAR!* on the other.

The crowd cheered, and even Lena stopped her twirling, stunned into silence. "Maggie Gallagher!" she squealed. "You're the best!"

Maggie's eyes shined with delight. "Oh, I love a good explosion."

So do I, answered her father in approval. *So do I.*

Children of all ages descended on the prizes, snatching up candy and noisemakers and throwing handfuls of confetti into the air. Even Mrs. Barrett from the post office scooped up a few banners. On Monday morning, they would be proudly displayed beside her cash register. Odawahaka was a town that had always loved its football. But now it seemed pretty fond of a six-foot mouse as well.

On Monday, Mr. Platt's daily Platt-itude had Maggie thinking.

Today he had written, *You don't have to learn. Ignorance is an option. Think about it.*

Maggie looked around. Were the other students "thinking about it," too? They didn't seem to be. Math was their last period of the day; most of the students seemed to be "thinking about" escape.

"Don't forget!" said Mr. Platt just as the final bell rang. "Tomorrow after school—another meeting of the Robotics Club. It's going to be awesome." *Poor Mr. Platt,* thought Maggie. Not one person had joined his club. When was he going to learn that he wasn't teaching at a school where kids signed up for anything except football?

"Your house or mine?" asked Lena as they walked out of the school.

"Depends," said Maggie. "What did your dad make for dinner last night?"

"Bouillabaisse," said Lena, "a classic French dish. In honor of my mom."

"Boo-ya-what?" asked Maggie.

"Fish stew," explained Lena. "Yummy."

"I've got powdered doughnuts at my house," said Maggie. "A whole box, unless Grandpop found them." Not likely, since Maggie had hidden them on top of the fridge behind a three-pack of paper towels.

"Decided!" said Lena. "Besides, we need to work out the details of the next hack, don't we? What's your final decision: timer or remote control?"

"It will have to be a timer," said Maggie, clearly dissatisfied. "We can't risk getting caught red-handed in school with an unidentified remote control."

For the remainder of the uphill walk home, Lena filled Maggie in on the latest news from her mother in Paris. It was all so elegant and foreign. Maggie couldn't help thinking how Lena's family was utterly unlike her own, especially when the girls reached the top of 3rd Street and found Grandpop sitting in his wheelchair on the porch, despite the cool mid-October air.

"Did you finish off the Cool Whip yesterday?" he barked at Lena before they were even inside the front gate.

"I sure did!" replied Lena. "Sorry, Maggie's Grandpop! Do you want me to walk down to Weis Market and buy you another can?"

"I don't want another one *now!*" complained Grandpop bitterly. "I wanted it *yesterday.* You eat more than any child I've ever met. Come sit down here and earn your keep by reading the sports page to me. I can't find my glasses."

Maggie knew that her grandfather had hidden his

reading glasses to get Lena to sit with him, and Lena knew it, too. It was impossible to comprehend, but the two of them actually enjoyed each other's company—though Grandpop took every opportunity to point out that Lena was going to eat his house right out from under him.

"Get us a couple of Moxies, eh, Maggie?" ordered her grandfather. "And see if you can find that box of doughnuts your mother smuggled in and hid from me."

Maggie didn't even bother to argue. She dropped her backpack at the foot of the stairs, listening to Lena laugh at something her grandfather said. Suddenly, she spied a package on the living room table wrapped in plain brown paper with a familiar label on it: Vinnie's Vintage Auto Parts. The package was open.

"Grandpop, what is this?" asked Maggie, carrying it outside. She could see that it contained the exact radio faceplate from a 1967 El Camino that she'd mailed out a week ago to someone in Stroudsburg. How had it found its way back here? She never included a return address on her labeling.

"Oh, Danny sent me that. A belated birthday present. Nice of him, huh? He says there's a website that sells old auto parts."

Maggie startled, nearly dropping the package to the floor.

"Be careful!" said Grandpop. "That's worth something! The website has everything, Danny says. Parts for Camaros, GTOs, Trans Ams, Cougars. All the stuff I used to collect." He leaned over to Lena. "Back when I was a young troublemaker." Lena smiled, but glanced nervously at Maggie. Grandpop turned back to her. "I want to take a look at it." She handed him the package. "No, not the faceplate. The website. I want to see what all the fuss is about."

Maggie looked at Lena. Lena looked at Maggie. Vinnie's Vintage Auto Parts paid for *everything*—the wiring, the electronic components, the confetti, the candy, the speakers, the paper lanterns—everything they needed to go on making trouble. Including the two thousand Ping-Pong balls that were currently netted and rigged above the podium on the auditorium stage at Oda M. Without Vinnie, there would be no more hacking.

"Grandpop," said Maggie, "we don't have internet."

"I know, but you jump on that other girl's internet. You know, the rich one you used to play with when you were little."

Maggie shook her head. It was true she'd figured out Kayla's family's password (goodasgold251) years ago, but she wasn't going to let her grandfather know that. "They changed their password. I don't know it anymore."

"Well, then I'll go to the library in Bloomsburg. I'll use that Google thing."

"Sure, Grandpop," said Maggie. There was no need to worry. He hadn't been out of Odawahaka since he lost his leg. And if he did make it to the library in Bloomsburg, he wouldn't know what to ask for.

"That's what I'll do," asserted Grandpop, slapping his good leg. "I will get myself to Bloomsburg."

There was an uncomfortable silence, until Lena broke it by saying, "And here's what *I'm* going to do. I'm going to Weis and get us *all* some Cool Whip. I bet it's incredible on top of powdered doughnuts!"

EIGHTEEN

THE NEXT DAY WAS THE SECOND Tuesday in October, and that meant one thing at Odawahaka Middle School: time for the annual assembly to kick off class elections. Usually, a class president was elected for each grade: fifth, sixth, seventh, and eighth. But since the sixth grade was the only class that was still at Oda M, theirs would be the only election this year.

And everyone knew who would win: Kayla.

Kayla was a shoo-in for three reasons. First, she had a magnetic quality that bordered on magic; people fell under her spell and couldn't get out. Second, because Kayla had won last year, she was the incumbent—which is a huge advantage in any election. And third, no one else was interested in running. Running for class office was a lot of work, and this year's sixth graders weren't particularly fired up, especially since they were the last class at Oda M. What was the point in leading a school that was doomed in a town that was dying? It was like being elected captain of the *Titanic* five minutes before the ship sank. No wonder Mr. Platt still didn't have a single member in his new Robotics Club. Why try?

Besides, everyone knew that class president was an empty honor. There was no real power. Nothing ever changed at the school, no matter who was elected.

Principal Shute stood at the podium speed-reading the election rules from the *Official Odawahaka Middle School Handbook for Student Elections.* He was clearly bored, and the students mirrored his attitude by slumping in their seats and staring at the ceiling. The five classroom teachers sat onstage, as they did at every assembly, and Kayla sat beside them, since she was the outgoing class president.

There were only two students in the audience who *were* paying attention: Maggie, who kept checking her watch, and Lena, who kept checking the light meter on her camera.

"Anyone who would like to be a candidate," said Principal Shute, reading as quickly as possible from the manual, "should submit his or her name by placing it in the official nomination envelope kept in each homeroom. You have until Friday at noon to submit your name for candidacy. On that afternoon, the official Election Board will gather the nomination envelopes from each homeroom and announce the official candidates on Monday morning. At that point, the campaign season, which will last precisely two weeks, will be under way. Candidates will be permitted to hang posters in the halls and cafeteria. Candidate speeches will be given the last Monday in October here in the auditorium."

"Why is he reading so fast?" asked Lena. "It's like his pants are on fire!"

Maggie checked her watch again. "I don't know. Maybe he's got somewhere important to go."

"Appropriate presentation attire is *required* for all candidates," continued the principal, rushing ahead. "Young ladies, skirts. Gentlemen, ties. *No exceptions.* The last Tuesday in October is Election Day. Voting will take place during homeroom, results will be tabulated by the Election Board during lunch, and the results will be announced at the end of the day."

Mr. Shute closed the official handbook. "And now we will hear a word from our outgoing president, Kayla Gold." He turned to Kayla, adding, "Quickly."

There was polite applause as Kayla walked across

the stage toward the podium. "Hi, everyone!" she said brightly. "I just want to say that being class president is *awesome* and you should really all think about running! It's so much fun! I mean, it's a *ton* of work. You really have to put in a lot of hours. I'm not kidding you. And giving the speech is kind of nerve-racking, I mean, if you're not used to talking in front of *the whole school.* And you have to write out your speech ahead of time, which is sort of like having an extra homework assignment. But it's great to be president, even though you have to stay after school a bunch of times and sit in on meetings with the teachers and Principal Shute, which sometimes run really long. But like I said, it's great, and you should all give it a try!" Kayla returned to her seat with a little extra swish in her walk.

Maggie leaned over and whispered to Lena, "That girl could talk George Washington out of running for president."

"Her talents are many," responded Lena. "Her genius is evil. This isn't what I call democracy."

Maggie looked at her watch again. She wasn't thinking so much about democracy. The whole assembly was moving much more quickly than she had expected. Timing. It was everything in a hack.

"Back to your classrooms!" announced Mr. Shute, so

abruptly that all the students and even the teachers were caught off guard.

"Maggie!" hissed Lena.

No, no, no, thought Maggie. *He can't possibly be done.* In the history of Odawahaka Middle School, there had never been an assembly that had lasted less than ten minutes.

"We have to stall!" hissed Lena.

"Improvisation is *your* department."

Mr. Shute flicked off the podium light as the teachers stood from their seats to exit the stage. Kayla smiled out at the audience, giving the sixth grade one last view of her gorgeous teeth. In a minute, the auditorium would be empty. And a hack—so carefully planned and executed—would die a lonely, invisible death. It could *not* be allowed to happen.

Lena raised her hand and said, "Excuse me, Mr. Shute? As the official class photographer, I'd like to take a few pictures."

"I don't think a class assembly to read a few rules requires a photo." He gathered up the handbook and turned to leave.

"Excuse me?" persisted Lena. "I . . . I have a question."

"What is it?"

"I would like to know . . ." Lena paused. "Hold on. I just forgot what I was going to ask. Does that ever happen to you?" Mr. Shute glared at her but made no reply. Lena looked at Maggie, but Maggie's mind was a complete blank. The students sat back down in their chairs, happy to avoid a few more minutes of math or science or Spanish.

"I was wondering . . . who . . . is on the Election Board this year?" Lena smiled. It was a good question.

"Well, of course, I am the chairman. And the two faculty positions this year are held by Mr. Platt and Mrs. Dornbusch." He smiled in the direction of the teachers on the stage, and Maggie could tell by the grimace on Mrs. Dornbusch's face that she had *not* volunteered for the honor. "Now, back to your classrooms. No idling. No misbehavior. No *talking.*"

"But Mr. Shute," said Lena. "Is . . . I mean, has . . ." She looked again at Maggie. Maggie tried to will herself to come up with a question, but the only thing that popped into her head was, *What This Country Needs Is Plenty of Moxie.* Useless!

Lena stumbled on. "Have there . . . I know! Have there always been three people on the Election Board?"

Mr. Shute gave her a strange look. "I would think so, though, of course, this is *my* first year here at

Odawahaka Middle School, as well. Perhaps Mrs. Dornbusch, as the *oldest* member of our staff, could answer that question." There was more than a hint of a sneer in his voice.

Mrs. Dornbusch refused to meet his gaze. "I don't know," she said offhandedly. "And honestly I don't care."

"Three is the number in the handbook, in any case," said Mr. Shute hurriedly. "So that's how it will be conducted under my chairmanship."

"But!" shouted Maggie, leaping to her feet. "Doesn't it also say that there will be two student members on the board?" She had actually read the *Official Odawahaka Middle School Handbook for Student Elections* back in fifth grade, being the kind of girl who likes to know the rules before she breaks them.

"Well, by the book, yes," said Mr. Shute, stuffing the handbook into the breast pocket of his jacket, "but my understanding is there haven't been student members for years due to a general lack of interest from the students themselves."

"But it's the *rule*," said Maggie, keeping her eyes on Principal Shute. How much time had gone by? How much time did they still need?

Timers! said her father in disgust. *Fallible. Unreliable. Impossible to predict.*

"Very well!" snapped Mr. Shute, his exasperation evident. "Two student volunteers. Anyone?"

Not one student raised a hand. Who would want to be on a committee with Principal Shute and the B-1 Bomber? It was enough to make any sixth grader crawl under the nearest rock.

"We'll do it!" said Lena. "Maggie and I!"

"Fine," said Mr. Shute. "And now, as I said, back to your classes."

"Wait!" said Lena. "One picture, Principal Shute! For the bulletin board. Smile!"

And that's when it happened. Two thousand Ping-Pong balls fell from the ceiling of the stage, pouring down on the podium, showering Principal Shute in a hailstorm of bouncing balls.

"What the H-E-?" sputtered the astonished principal.

A cry rose up from the students. It was like seeing an unexpected fireworks display, or suddenly finding your-self at Knoebels Amusement Park when your parents had said you were going to visit your boring aunt Irma.

Mrs. Dornbusch nearly fell out of her seat laughing. She laughed so hard she had to remove her glasses and wipe the tears from her face. Mrs. Matlaw, however, was desperately concerned that the students were going to slip. She rushed forward to rescue them and promptly fell on her own rear end. Mr. Platt scuttled quickly to help her up.

"Look!" said Becky, holding up one of the white Ping-Pong balls. "It says 'ROAR!'"

"The Mouse is in the house!" shouted Max, and the others joined in. "The Mouse is in the house! The Mouse is in the House!" Students began to throw the Ping-Pong balls *at* each other, which added to the absurd mayhem.

"Silence!" shouted Mr. Shute, and even though the students quieted down, the balls continued to roll aimlessly across the floor, making a gentle sound, like the rustling of dry leaves, which calmed everybody down. A hush fell, as if they were in church and the service was about to begin.

"You will stay and pick up every single one of these balls," barked Mr. Shute. One of the boys snickered.

"These balls are not a joke!" shouted the principal. Several more students began to laugh, unable to hold it in.

"Balls are not a laughing matter!" By this time, the entire sixth grade had dissolved into uncontrollable giggles.

Lena and Maggie gave each other a secret low-five, tickling fingers rather than slapping so as not to draw attention to themselves.

"This shall forever be known as the Epic Balls-on-Shute Hack," said Lena.

"And no matter what," said Maggie, "it will not be forgotten."

NINETEEN

LATER, IN THE CAFETERIA, THE CONVERSATION at Table 10 kept bouncing back and forth between the elections and the Mouse. Eventually Lyle, slowly munching on the cafeteria's infamous Crispy Fish Sandwich, said, "The Mouse should run for class president."

There was a moment of silence before everyone (except Kayla) burst out laughing.

"I would totally vote for the Mouse!" shouted Max.

"So would I," said Tyler. Jenna nodded in agreement.

"The Mouse can't be president," said Kayla, "because the Mouse doesn't exist!" She tossed her hair, as if that ended the discussion.

"The Mouse exists," said Lyle. "We just don't know who it is."

"Is it YOU?" shouted Tyler dramatically, pointing a celery stick at Becky, who was at the next table over. "Or YOU?" as he turned the vegetable on Grace. Both girls giggled, which Maggie found really annoying.

"Sometimes I feel like the Mouse is all of us," said Jenna quietly. Her voice faltered. "I don't know . . ."

"Jenna is right!" said Lena. "The Mouse is every one of us. Standing up to injustice. Battling the forces of evil. Giving a voice to the silent, the downtrodden, the huddled masses yearning to breathe free." She stood up and held her carton of milk aloft.

"Eating garbage!" said Lyle, standing and holding his sandwich high.

"Avoiding mousetraps," said Maggie, standing and holding up her half-eaten chocolate chip cookie.

"Leaving mouse poop everywhere!" added Tyler, standing and brandishing his sandwich bun as if he were waving a battle flag.

"Young scholars!" said Mr. Esposito mildly, approaching with his arms outstretched. "Perhaps a little less volume from your table."

"We're starting a revolution, Mr. Esposito," said Lena cheerfully.

"Ah, *imperium in imperio*," said Mr. Esposito, smiling broadly. "An empire within an empire. Well, finish your lunch first. You can't fight the good fight on an empty stomach."

"Mr. Esposito?" said Lena. "How do you say, 'I am the Mouse' in Latin?"

Mr. Esposito's smile grew. "That would be *Sum mus,* both spelled with a single *u* but pronounced as if a double *o. Soom moose.* Or, if you wanted to add some emphasis, you could say, *Mus, sum,* that is, 'The Mouse, I am!'" Here, he raised his hand in a regal flourish such as one that Caesar might have made as he crossed the Rubicon with his army.

As soon as the words were out of his mouth, though, the smile dropped from his lips. "I, ah, wouldn't go around saying that today, though. No, no." He quickly looked around him as he began to fiddle with his tie. "I, ah, wouldn't think it wise. No, no. Not wise. *Vox populi, vox nihili,* you know." He hurried off, shaking his head as if he regretted that Caesarian salute.

"The Mouse can*not* be class president, because the Mouse is *not* a person," hissed Kayla, angry enough to spit nails. "It's just a stupid joke, and Principal Shute is going to figure out who is behind it, and when he does, that person will be *expelled.*" She picked up her tray and walked away from the table.

"What's got her so worked up?" asked Colt.

Lyle nibbled on his napkin like a rabbit nibbling on a leaf of lettuce. "She knows she's only got one real challenger in the campaign. And it's imaginary." He paused for a moment. "And has a tail."

Maggie was beginning to see that Lena liked to *push things*. Ideas. Boundaries. People. Maggie in particular.

"I get it," Maggie said, holding up her hands in defense against Lena's onslaught. They were walking home after school, and Lena wouldn't let go of the idea of a Mouse campaign. "It's an interesting question: How do you get a candidate elected that doesn't even exist? And it would be *challenging* to try to figure out the answer. I just don't see how we're going to get past step one."

Lena persisted. "How hard can it be to stick a name in an envelope? Mrs. I.D.C., remember?"

"It's Kayla I'm worried about. She's going to keep her eye on that nomination envelope like a heat-seeking missile locked on a target. And even if we slip it past her—so what? Mr. Shute will just tear it up."

"But *we're* on the Election Board. And so is Mr. Platt. Mr. Shute can't just tear up a name on his own. If he does . . . there'll be an uprising!"

"An uprising? Where do you *come* from? This is

Odawahaka. People don't just *rise up*. Unless Weis runs out of Cocoa Puffs."

"C'mon," said Lena. "Let's give it a try. Just to see what *happens*."

They were at the top of 3rd Street. Grandpop was on the front porch. It was colder than yesterday, and he had an old plaid blanket thrown over his lap. Maggie was surprised to see him outside. Waiting. Waiting for them.

She was embarrassed to admit, even to herself, how nice it felt to have someone waiting at the top of the hill.

Inside every large problem . . . , whispered her father.

Oh, shush, thought Maggie, but she smiled.

"You're smiling," said Lena, dancing in a circle around her. "That's your 'I'm working on a problem' smile."

"It is not," argued Maggie. But it was, and she wondered at the fact that Lena had learned such a thing about her, in just a few short weeks.

TWENTY

"WE WILL MAKE THIS QUICK, AS I have an extremely important meeting off-site in less than an hour." Principal Shute stood at the door of the school's conference room, his cell phone in his hand and a look of disinterest on his face.

Mrs. Dornbusch had commandeered the chair at the foot of the table, which allowed her some extra legroom and the chance to distance herself from the proceedings.

"This is exciting, huh?" asked Mr. Platt, as eager as a puppy before his food bowl is filled. "My first election! I wonder who the candidates will be. I've gathered the envelopes from the other teachers. Mrs. Dornbusch, did you bring yours?"

Without a word, Mrs. Dornbusch slapped down the envelope that had been tacked to her bulletin board for the past three days, then gave it a shove so that it skidded to a stop in front of Mr. Platt. It was clear she hadn't bothered to look inside.

"How do we do this?" asked Mr. Platt. "Is there a protocol?"

"Just read the names," said Mr. Shute, glancing at his phone. "Our student members can take notes, and then I'll have the list typed up by Mrs. McDermott for tomorrow's morning announcements. Excuse me," he said, standing up. "This is a call I need to take." Without looking back, he walked out of the room.

"Exciting!" said Mr. Platt again.

"I've got a notebook," said Maggie. "I'll write down the names."

"And I'll take a picture of each slip of paper," said Lena. "As an official record. Evidence that everything was done fairly."

Mr. Platt chuckled. "I don't think we need to worry about anything *underhanded* going on here." He looked at Mrs. Dornbusch and said, "Underhanded: an eleven-letter word for devious." There was a bit of a crow in his voice. Jelly beans were piling up in his office. "But record away!" he said to Lena. "Let posterity know that the Election Board cannot be corrupted!"

"Oh, cool your jets, Paul," said Mrs. Dornbusch,

retying her sneaker on the edge of the table. "There's probably just one name submitted. Oda M isn't exactly a beehive of student involvement." She snapped the end of her shoelace to show her irritation with the energetic math teacher.

But it turned out there were three names in the first envelope alone. And then one in the next, and one in the third. The fourth envelope had two more names, so that by the time Mr. Platt opened Mrs. Dornbusch's envelope—the fifth and final one—there were already seven candidates, which was seven times the number of nominations last year.

"This is so great!" exclaimed Mr. Platt. "Just the kind of school I'd always hoped to teach at! Energy! Activism! Let's see who's throwing their hat into the ring from Mrs. Dornbusch's class." He pulled out three folded slips of paper.

Maggie knew two of them, but she had no idea who the third belonged to. She couldn't have been more surprised when Mr. Platt read out loud, "Colt DuPrey."

Colt? The boy who spent more time reading books about kids battling mythological gods than actually talking to kids in real life? That Colt DuPrey?

"Why would Colt want to run for class president?" Maggie asked, the question escaping her lips before she realized she was talking out loud.

Bad habit, whispered her father.

But Lena smiled and mouthed the word *ROAR*.

Maggie wrote the name down on the list, and Lena photographed it for the official record.

Mr. Shute reappeared, tucking his cell phone into his pocket with an enigmatic smile on his face. Mr. Platt pulled out the second slip of paper and read it out loud: "Kayla Gold." He held up the slip of paper for Lena to photograph.

"And . . ." Mr. Platt unfolded the final slip of paper, then stopped, frozen, as if frightened in a way that teachers should never be. Mr. Shute stared at his newest teacher, and a vision popped into Maggie's head of a hawk that has sighted a hairless, blind, utterly helpless, newborn mouse.

In that instant, Maggie saw the flaw in the design of this hack. She had missed this possibility: that a teacher could be vulnerable, too.

This is where things fall apart.

Mr. Platt took a deep breath. "The Mouse," he said evenly, and held up the slip of paper for Lena to photograph.

Click.

"Got it!" said Lena exuberantly.

Maggie's pen quickly scribbled the name at the end of the list of candidates. She ripped the page from her notebook and stood up. "I'll give the list to Mrs. McDermott."

"Stop!" shouted Mr. Shute (which was in fact what Mrs. Dornbusch called him: Principal Shout). "Let me see that slip of paper," he said to Mr. Platt. He scrutinized the writing, then carefully folded the paper and placed it in his pocket. "Scratch that last name from the list, Maggie, and give the list to Mrs. McDermott."

"But the name was submitted," said Maggie. "Like all the others."

"The Mouse is not a student at Odawahaka Middle School."

Mrs. Dornbusch snorted. "Do you think it's a teacher? We're a shifty bunch. Just the kind that would try to crash a student election."

Mr. Platt turned to Mr. Shute. "I think what Mrs. Dornbusch is trying to say—"

"I know what I'm trying to say," snapped Mrs. Dornbusch. "Don't be a suck-up, Paul."

"—is that perhaps one of the students at the school is trying to find a way to participate more fully in the activities and social flow, but hasn't quite found a way to do that without a 'persona' of some kind. It's actually very common at this age. *Alter Egos in the Development of the Adolescent Psyche*. It was my master's thesis—"

Mr. Shute held up a hand to silence his math teacher. "Don't care. No mouse," he said, glancing again at his phone. "Decision. Done. Final."

"But that isn't democracy," said Lena.

Mr. Shute smiled, then chuckled. Then he began to laugh.

Maggie was furious. She knew that democracy had no place in middle school, but Lena still *believed*. And Maggie wasn't about to let a blockhead like Mr. Shute ruin her friend's dreams of a better world. "Are you afraid the Mouse will win?" asked Maggie, staring straight at the principal.

His laughter ended abruptly. "Afraid of a rodent?" Mr. Shute narrowed his eyes at Maggie. "I've seen men die in combat. I'm not afraid of a mouse." His phone rang again. He glanced at the screen and took the call, turning his back on the others.

"Then let's put it to a vote," said Mr. Platt. "Those in favor of allowing all the names to be on the ballot, raise your hand." Maggie, Lena, and Mr. Platt raised their hands. "All opposed?" Mr. Shute waved his hand over his head.

"I don't care," said Mrs. Dornbusch. "I just want to

go home." She stood and started to walk to the door.

"The *ayes* carry the day," said Mr. Platt. "The complete list goes to Mrs. McDermott."

Maggie hurried past Principal Shute, who was still talking on the phone. Even so, he managed to snap the list out of her hand and said, "*I* will give the list to Mrs. McDermott," before returning to his conversation.

As Mrs. Dornbusch exited, Maggie heard her mutter to Mr. Platt, "You're such a fool."

On Monday morning during homeroom, Mrs. Dornbusch was shopping online for socks. At one point, she called Maggie and Lena over to her desk. "Lena and . . ." She paused, stumped. "Not Madeleine. Not Mandy. Not Marissa."

"My name is—"

"Stop," interrupted the Barn Stormer. "I have something more important to discuss." Her eyes remained glued to her computer screen. "Principal Shute is going to begin the morning announcements in less than a minute. You are both young. Which means you are stupid. Don't do anything stupid. That's all I have to say." She waved them away and continued with her online shopping.

Maggie bridled at the accusation of stupidity. "What

do you care if we do something stupid?" she challenged.

Mrs. Dornbusch still didn't look up from her screen. "Because it will require more meetings of that hideous Election Board." She pointed at the blackboard, where her chalk countdown number read *150.* "Take my advice. Just. Give. Up."

Maggie and Lena drifted back to their seats. "Boy," said Lena. "She needs to go on a vacation. Like, forever." Maggie didn't say anything, but she could tell the Gray Gargoyle knew something they didn't.

Kayla wandered over to where Lena and Maggie were sitting. "Hi, guys," she said, flashing a smile and twisting one strand of her perfect hair around an index finger. "I guess a lot of kids signed up this year."

"We're not allowed to talk about it," said Maggie.

"Oh, right," said Kayla. "It's just kind of weird, don't you think? So many people wanting to run? No one ever runs." Maggie had never heard Kayla's voice sound like this before: *mousy.* "Well!" She seemed to rally. "I hope I can count on *your* support. I'm definitely the most quali-fied candidate and—"

"Kayla, you don't have to campaign with me," said Maggie flatly. "I *know* you. Remember?"

"Oh, yeah. Right. Since kindergarten." Kayla seemed to deflate a little, and Maggie couldn't figure out what was going on. When had Kayla ever cared about Maggie's support?

"I'm sure you'll be a great candidate!" said Lena. Just then, the *ping!* of the morning announcement tone sounded, and Kayla hurried back to her seat, an unmasked look of dread on her face.

Following the Pledge of Allegiance and five seconds of silent reflection, Principal Shute got right down to business: "Normally I would announce the names of the candidates for class president this morning, but we've had an unprecedented number of students submit their names, and so I made an executive decision to add one more step to the election process. I have decided to require each candidate to gather at least ten signatures on an official petition paper in order to be included on the ballot. At this time, any student who submitted a name for nomination may proceed to the main office to receive an official petition. The signed petitions must be delivered to Mrs. McDermott by the end of school *today*. No exceptions."

Maggie looked at Lena. Lena looked at Maggie. How could they possibly gather signatures in less than six hours when they couldn't even go to the office to collect the official petition paper?

"Mrs. Dornbusch?" asked Kayla. "May I please go to the office to get my petition paper?" She was smiling, her usual confidence restored. Mrs. Dornbusch waved her away impatiently. She was bidding on eBay for a pair of argyles.

"Anyone else going?" Kayla glanced around the room. Colt stood up slowly, carefully marking the page in his book, and moved toward the door. "Colt! Guess it's just us, then!" Kayla couldn't have been happier. She scooped up her books and marched out the door, a slight bounce in her walk that made her shiny hair dance.

"Mrs. Dornbusch?" asked Lena, gathering up her books. "Maggie and I need to photocopy something for the Robotics Club meeting tomorrow. Can we go to the office now, instead of during lunch?"

Mrs. Dornbusch waved them away, but Maggie was pretty sure she heard the B-1 Bomber mutter, "And so it begins. . . ."

As they hurried up the stairs, Maggie said to Lena, "Mrs. McDermott isn't going to give us a petition paper."

"Well, not with *that* attitude," said Lena, two steps ahead of her.

"Lena, this isn't a question of attitude. We need a *plan*."

"So we'll make up a plan as we go," said Lena, punching her way through the double doors at the top of the stairwell.

"I hate the way you make things up on the fly!" said

Maggie, even though she had to admit that Lena was a pretty impressive wing nut.

When they got to the office, a cluster of students was waiting to pick up their papers. Kayla stood at the very front of the line.

"Excuse me, Mrs. McDermott," said Lena, holding up a blank lab report from chemistry class. "Mrs. Dornbusch needs one hundred copies of this before first period. She asked if we would do it, because she's very busy preparing for class."

"I'm busy, too!" said Mrs. McDermott sharply. "With completely unnecessary paperwork, if you ask me." She didn't even lower her voice, although the door to Mr. Shute's office was wide open. "Go ahead. I filled the paper tray this morning."

"What *are* we doing?" whispered Maggie.

"I have no idea! Just look like we're getting ready to make copies," said Lena, lifting the cover of the copier. "We'll think of something!"

Maggie and Lena fussed with the positioning of the blank lab report, watching as Kayla received her official petition paper. They needed to get their hands on that petition before anyone signed it.

Flattery! hissed Maggie's father. *It works with insecure people every time. . . .*

Maggie paused. Insecure? What was her father talking about? But there wasn't time to think. She walked over to Kayla and said, "Hey! Can I be the *first* to sign your petition?"

"Absolutely!" Kayla flashed her megawatt smile—it was, after all, campaign season—and handed her paper to Maggie.

"I just have to get my pen out of my backpack," said Maggie.

"I have a pen," said Kayla, holding out a pink gel pen.

Maggie wrinkled her nose. "You know, Kayla, pink is just *not* my thing. I'll get my own."

She walked over to the copy machine and slipped the blank petition into the feeder. "Distract her!" Maggie said to Lena.

But Kayla didn't need any distracting, she was so busy chatting up the other candidates. "I guarantee you," said Lena. "She'll win some of *their* votes."

Less than a minute later, Maggie returned the petition to Kayla. Kayla looked at Maggie's signature and smiled.

"This is the best, Maggie," said Kayla, and Maggie could almost believe she meant it, almost remember what it was like when they were best friends. Kayla was that good at faking.

When Maggie returned to the copy machine, Lena had already slipped the copies of the petition, each listing THE MOUSE as the candidate, into her backpack.

"You crazy master of improvisation," said Lena.

Wing nut, said her father, but Maggie couldn't tell if he meant it as an insult or a compliment.

TWENTY-ONE

LENA CALLED THEIR FIRST STRATEGY Operation Sea Turtle. They would blanket the walls with petitions, immediately rescuing any that had even one signature, in the hopes that sheer numbers would result in a few survivors.

"We don't have tape!" said Lena, in a panic.

Maggie gave her a flat look. "I'm an engineer. I *always* have tape." She produced three kinds from her backpack: duct, masking, and simple Scotch.

But not one petition survived to the end of first period. Mr. Shute had removed them all.

"We need a different strategy," said Lena. They decided to adopt Operation Quail, camouflaging the petitions by placing them on crowded bulletin boards where they would blend in with their surroundings, thus avoiding Mr. Shute's detection. But apparently the petitions blended in so well that nobody noticed them at all.

"This is hopeless," said Maggie by the time lunch began. The other candidates had already collected their signatures and returned their petitions to Mrs. McDermott. It appeared that the list of candidates was complete. "We haven't got even one signature, and we're down to our *last* blank petition paper."

"*Think*," said Lena. "This is what you do best, Maggie. Don't give up now! Remember what your dad wrote in his notebook: 'Inside every large problem is a small problem struggling to get out.'"

"They're all big problems," grumbled Maggie. "We need to think of a place where lots of kids *go*, but Mr. Shute *can't go*." She slowly tapped her index finger against her lips. "A place where kids go. *Where kids go*." She started to laugh. "Oh no. No! It's too easy. *Way* too easy."

By the time lunch ended, the Mouse's "campaign team" had taped the final blank petition paper on the inside of the first stall door in the girls' bathroom on the sixth-grade hallway. By the end of fifth period, they had over twenty signatures. What was surprising was that one of the signatures belonged to Lyle. There was also a small bite taken out of the paper. When it came to doing things his own way, Lyle was in a league of his own.

"Have you figured out how we're going to get the petition delivered to Mrs. McDermott—before the last bell?" asked Lena.

"Done," said Maggie. "We just need to tape the envelope to the underside of the school mascot. I've already arranged for the pickup and delivery." Inside her head, Maggie offered words of gratitude. *Thank you, Vinnie.* She paused. *And thanks, Grandpop.* Without his old pile of junk, none of this would have been possible.

Five minutes before the final bell rang, as Lena and Maggie sat in Mrs. Matlaw's class, their eyes nervously on the clock, there was a ruckus in the hallway. Shouting could be heard, and the shouting clearly belonged to Principal Shute.

"Children," said Mrs. Matlaw, moving quickly but smoothly to the open classroom door, "stay in your seats." She walked out into the hallway. "Holy schnitzel!" she exclaimed, which was the closest thing to an expletive that anyone had ever heard come out of Mrs. Matlaw's mouth. Within seconds, the entire classroom emptied into the hallway.

Principal Shute was shouting at a human-sized mouse: "Trespassing! Breaking and entering! Threatening children!"

189

"Look, Bud," said the mouse, giving it back as good as it got. "This school is public grounds. I was *buzzed* in by your secretary. And I haven't even seen a kid, so I don't know what gives you the right to say I'm threatening one!" The mouse looked around. By now the hallway was filled with every sixth grader in the school. "Oh, hey, kids!" said the mouse, cheerfully waving with one hand. The other hand held an enormous bunch of helium balloons in every color: lilac, lemon, rose, sky blue. They looked like a floating springtime bouquet.

"I won't have this disruption!" screamed Mr. Shute.

"Then stop making so much noise," suggested the mouse. "Look, I was hired to deliver these balloons along with this card." Maggie could still see the pieces of tape that she'd used to attach the envelope to the belly of the Wildcats statue. "And if you'll just let me do my job, I'll get out of your hair."

"Fine," said Mr. Shute. "Give them to me."

"No-o-o," said the mouse. "I was told, very specifically, to hand these over to Mrs. McDermott—and *only* Mrs. McDermott."

"They're for me?" asked Mrs. McDermott, who had been standing in the doorway to the main office. "But it isn't my birthday or . . ." She reached forward, unable to resist the colorful, joyful effervescence of the balloons.

Mr. Shute advanced as though to block the delivery, but the mouse sidestepped the principal and made the handoff to Mrs. McDermott. In the tangle of the transfer, though, the balloon bouquet slipped between them. It started to float, higher and higher, toward the rotunda, which rose fifty feet above the ground.

Lyle—in an act of pure heroism, complete recklessness, and surprising speed—scrambled onto the back of the Wildcats mascot, jumped into the air, and grabbed the balloons before they floated out of reach. The sixth graders cheered as he walked back to Mrs. McDermott, who had just finished reading the card, and handed them to her.

"You know what, Mrs. McDermott?" Lyle said. "Even if it isn't your birthday, you deserve these balloons, because you're one of the nicest people in the whole town."

Mrs. McDermott stared at Lyle, and tears began to sparkle in her eyes. "Well. Well, now. That is the sweetest thing that anyone has ever said to me." Everyone cheered for the school secretary, who had kept Oda M running, even after the rest of the town had practically abandoned their school.

"The day isn't over, Mrs. McDermott," said Mr. Shute sternly, "and you have abandoned your post!"

"But I have official duties to perform, Principal Shute," said Mrs. McDermott, unflappable as usual. "I have an announcement to make to the entire school, and since we're all assembled, I will make it now: the Mouse is officially a candidate for class president." She held up the signed petition, which had been tucked inside the card. Applause erupted from the students.

"We're on the ballot," whispered Maggie to Lena. Was it her imagination, or did Principal Shute single them out of the crowd and pin them with a particularly venomous stare?

As the final bell rang, Kayla turned on her heel and walked stiffly past both Maggie and Lena to retrieve her backpack from the classroom. On her way out, she passed them again and said in a voice so sharp you could have cut paper with it, "I don't care if Santa Claus himself is on the ballot. I'm going to win this election, and I *will* be the last class president this school ever has."

"*Yikes*," whispered Lena to Maggie after Kayla had walked off.

"You have no idea," said Maggie, shaking her head. "We just bought ourselves a world of trouble."

TWENTY-TWO

"HOW MANY POSTERS SHOULD WE RUN OFF?" asked Lena. They had spent the afternoon at Lena's house, eating cappuccino crunch ice cream and designing campaign posters for the Mouse. Lena's house not only had better ice cream flavors—black raspberry swirl, butter brickle, pistachio chocolate chip—it also had her large-format printer. The only ice cream at Maggie's house was Hoodsie cups, which Grandpop sometimes dropped by the spoonful into a tall glass of Moxie, calling it a Brown Cow. And Maggie's printer was so old she couldn't even get the ink cartridges for it anymore, except by special order.

"Ten each," said Maggie. They'd ended up with two versions they liked.

The first poster showed the American flag waving proudly. But when you looked closely at the image, you could see that the red stripes were made up of dozens of tiny photographs of every sixth grader at Oda M—the photographs that Lena had been taking since school began. Everyone was represented. No one was left out. And right in the center of the field of stars was the face of the Mouse. The message on the poster was: E PLURIBUS UNUM. Out of many, one.

The other poster was a masterpiece, in Maggie's opinion. Lena had used a photograph of a famous baseball player hitting a home run and Photoshopped the head of a mouse on the baseball player's body. The message read, *Everyone deserves a turn AT BAT.* Maggie liked this poster even more, because it took aim at Principal Shute. Every sixth grader would know that the Mouse was standing up to the autocratic principal at Oda M.

"Let's go for twenty each!" said Lena. "I want to *cover* the school."

"You think big," said Maggie, shaking her head as if she thought it was both a good thing and a bad thing.

"Yeah," said Lena. "And there's something else I've been thinking about, too. Don't you think it's time we let a few more people in on the whole Mouse thing?"

"A few more people? Like who?"

"Well . . . like the whole class."

"What?"

A wing nut, said her father. *I told you from the beginning. . . .*

"I don't mean we tell them that we started the Mouse. But we let them be a part of it." Lena looked at Maggie as if she understood that what she was saying sounded completely crazy—but she believed it anyway. "Because now that the Mouse is running for class president, it's not just a hack anymore. It's a movement."

"*Just* a hack?" said Maggie. "JUST a hack?"

"I don't mean it like that. Hacking is great. It's fun. It's clever. But sometimes one thing grows into something else—something bigger. The Mouse has something to say."

"The Mouse doesn't even exist!" yelled Maggie. "It's just something I made up because I wanted to see if I could actually stuff two hundred tennis balls into a locker. And you know what? I did. *That* was a great hack. It made people laugh. It made people scratch their heads and say, 'How did they do that?' And it was original. It had never been done before. At least not at Oda M."

Maggie felt sick from eating too much ice cream, and the smell of the ink from the large-format printer was giving her a headache, too. She didn't feel well, and she did not want to be having this argument with Lena.

But she couldn't stop it now that it had started.

"You always do this," Maggie said. "You always want everything to have some big *message* or *cause* or *revolution*. I don't know about where you come from, but in Odawahaka, we kind of just live our lives, you know? We're not always out to change the world."

"I thought you wanted to change Odawahaka!" said Lena.

"No! I want to get out. I want to leave this town. I want to go to college far away from here and never come back."

"I know," said Lena angrily. "That's pretty much the first thing you told me when we met." She picked up her camera and began to fiddle with the knobs, keeping her eyes down. "I just thought . . . well, anyway. I thought you might want the Mouse to be more than just a silly hack."

Maggie stiffened. "Hacking is not silly." Inside her head, she added, *My* dad *was not silly.* She felt flushed and a little dizzy, the ice cream in her stomach threatening to make a guest appearance all over the floor. She couldn't believe that Lena was saying these things about her father. That he was unimportant. That he didn't care about grand causes and big ideas. It was almost like she was saying that he hadn't existed at all.

"You don't get it," continued Maggie. "You never did. I don't know why I even let you know anything . . . about him. About me. About any of this."

"Him?" asked Lena, still angry. "Who are you even talking about?"

"I showed you . . ." Maggie couldn't believe she had actually showed Lena her father's notebooks. They were the most private thing in her life. "We were fine before you came to town, you know. Just fine. We never needed you." She picked up her backpack and ran out.

By the time Maggie banged through the gate of her own house, she had wiped the tears from her face.

"What's the hurry?"

"Nothing, Grandpop," said Maggie, hiding her face as she headed for the stairs. The TV was on, filling the room with its sickly blue light and the irritating hum of scripted excitement.

"Where's your friend?" Grandpop pivoted in his wheelchair, turning away from the TV to track her as she climbed the stairs.

"Home. Not here. Who cares? She doesn't come over *every* day."

"Well, pretty near every day. Or you go over there. Seems like you two are cats with your tails tied together. And the way that girl eats! It's like nothing I've ever seen! Not a single Wheat Thin left in the house."

"Well, don't worry. Your Wheat Thins are safe. She won't be coming around anymore."

"Oh," said Grandpop quietly. He shifted in his chair. "You had a fight?"

"*She* had a fight. I just happened to be in the room." Maggie sat down at the bottom of the stairs and rested her head in her hand.

"Hmm." He rubbed his stump of a leg, the one half taken by disease. Maggie stared at it and imagined her grandfather being eaten alive by sickness. The lump of ice cream in her stomach turned over. She stood up abruptly.

"I'm going upstairs, Grandpop."

"Well, hold on, there. Who's making dinner?" he asked. "Your mother hasn't come home yet, and who knows what time she'll get in?"

"I'm not hungry," said Maggie. She picked up her backpack and turned to go upstairs.

"Well, that doesn't mean I'm not! And I'm tired of heating up cans of soup. Come in the kitchen with me. We'll scrounge up something."

"I don't feel like—"

"Get!" he said, pointing to the kitchen. Maggie did as she was told.

After a thorough review of every cupboard, shelf, and the refrigerator, both Maggie and her grandfather agreed there was absolutely nothing to eat in the entire house.

"What kind of a mother have you got?" asked Grandpop, as if her mother wasn't in any way, shape, or form related to him, too.

"She's busy. She works," said Maggie, slumped at the kitchen table with her head in her hands. She wasn't used to defending her mother, but Grandpop's refusal to allow her to retreat to her room made her feel like picking a fight. "You know, you could go to the store, too. The van can pick you up and bring you back, Tuesdays and Thursdays."

"Your grandmom did the grocery shopping," said Grandpop definitively.

"Well, hear the news. Grandmom isn't here anymore." Maggie was tired. Her stomach still felt floppy, and she desperately wanted to lie down in the quiet of her room.

Her grandfather pushed himself farther away in his wheelchair as if he needed to distance himself to see her properly. "What a wicked thing to say."

Maggie flipped through the pile of mail on the kitchen table. Junk. Junk. Junk. What a surprise. She could feel that bad part of her taking over, the part she didn't want anyone to see. She knew she should care about Grandpop's feelings, but right now she didn't. He was right. She was wicked. And she couldn't stop. "You know, sometimes I think how lucky Grandmom was . . . getting out."

"Really?" said Grandpop, wheeling his chair away from her. "Lucky? Your grandmom loved this town. And she loved me. And hear *this* news: She loved you, too. So if you've got some romantic notion in that addled head of yours that being *dead* is better than being in Odawahaka, then I think you might want to keep that ugly thought to yourself."

Maggie stared at her grandfather, still in the iron grip of anger, but ashamed of herself and how she'd behaved—and not knowing how to say *I'm sorry.*

Yes, explosions *are* a fact of life.

Which is why Maggie turned and threw up all over the kitchen floor.

TWENTY-THREE

"I'M SORRY." LENA STOOD IN THE doorway of Maggie's bedroom. It was dark out now, but Maggie didn't know what time it was. No one had called her for dinner. She had fallen asleep and been surprised to hear the knocking on her bedroom door and even more surprised to see Lena standing on the other side when she opened up.

Maggie rubbed her face. Her hair had taken on the appearance of a dandelion gone to seed—springy and puffed out. She could feel a strand of it stuck in her mouth. She raked her fingers over her tongue until she finally snagged the hair and extracted it, wiping her saliva-covered fingers on her jeans. She turned away from Lena and went back to her bed. While she'd been sleeping, she'd accidentally knocked the box with her father's things to the floor, and all the contents had spilled out. She knelt down to gather the notebooks, photos, and newspaper clippings.

"I didn't mean to get you all upset like that," said Lena, following her. "I don't even know what I said, but it doesn't matter because I *did* get you upset and I'm really, really sorry. Do you want to talk about it?" She crouched down next to Maggie and reached out to help gather the contents of the box.

"Don't touch it!" said Maggie. "Don't . . . touch . . . anything." She continued to organize and straighten the papers. There were so few of them, really. Her head felt like it was stuffed with mashed potatoes.

Lena sat down on the floor, cross-legged. She didn't seem angry, which was hard for Maggie to understand. In Maggie's house, angry words followed angry words. And sometimes there was vomiting. But Lena seemed almost calm.

Maggie put the last scrap of paper back in the box. "That's everything I know about my dad. Everything. In that box." She nudged the box with her foot. "I've spent years looking on the internet. I've asked my mom. But that's it. That's every last thing I know about him."

"It's not a whole lot," said Lena, looking at the photo on the top of the pile.

Maggie shook her head. "It's not enough. It'll never

be enough." She pushed her hair back, wondering if she might catch the sound of her father whispering in her ear, but there was nothing. He was slipping away. Maggie tried hard to find a way to put this fear into words. "Sometimes I think I hack because it helps me feel like he's near. It helps me feel like he's still alive. But there isn't enough," she said, nudging the box again, "to keep him alive. And my mom won't talk about him, ever. So when I read through his notes and then I follow his instructions, it's like he's still . . . being my dad."

Lena nodded thoughtfully. "I get what you're saying. It's kind of like how I keep rearranging my mom's glass-blowing stuff. You know, move it around, so it doesn't just *sit* there. So it feels like she's still in the house. Not so far away."

That should have made Maggie feel better, to know that she wasn't the only one who had to work to pull a parent closer.

But tonight, all she could feel was the differences, the things that made her and Lena seem like complete opposites. The hair, the height, the style, the vision, the mission, the way of looking at the world. Maggie thought again of the unkind things she had said to her grandfather, and she knew that Lena would never say such things—to anyone.

A question popped into Maggie's scientist brain, and she asked it without thinking. "How did we get to be friends?"

Lena opened her eyes wide in surprise, as if she couldn't believe that Maggie didn't know the answer. "I chose you," she said. "That very first day of school. You were the Girl Hiding in the Bushes. You were the Girl with the Secret Package. I took one look at you and said to myself, 'That girl isn't like everyone else. That girl does things her own way. And *that's* my new best friend.'" Lena laughed and threw up her hands. "You were doomed, absolutely doomed, from that moment on."

Maggie was speechless. To be seen, really seen. To be understood. And still chosen? It seemed like a miracle to her—that is, if she'd been the kind of girl who believed in miracles. Believing in miracles, though— that was Lena's department.

In the end, the girls decided to do it Lena's way. It was time for the Mouse to be more than a hack. Or perhaps to be the greatest hack that had ever been pulled off.

Instead of sneaking into the school through the rusted rear door, Lena and Maggie had decided to ask the sixth graders to do their part. But would they?

Would they get involved? Would they care? Enough?

People almost always let you down, grumbled Maggie's father as the girls crept through the sleeping town at five o'clock in the morning.

But Maggie had decided to trust Lena, and Lena was sure this hack would work. "Strength in numbers," Lena said with confidence. "I believe."

"Okay," said Maggie, trying to have some faith, too.

Maggie and Lena crept along empty streets, each carrying a bundle of tightly rolled posters tied with string.

"Whose house is this?" asked Lena, whispering as they approached a tidy two-story house on Berger Avenue. The porch was covered in Halloween decorations, with several blowing ghosts hanging in a straight row as if they were trying out for the Rockettes. A giant furry spider the size of a Hula Hoop leaned against the carport.

"Jenna's," said Maggie. She quietly tiptoed onto the porch and left a rolled-up poster on the plastic table by the door. The poster was tied with a bright red ribbon that had a note attached to it:

WILL YOU PLEASE HANG THIS POSTER FOR ME?
YOUR FRIEND AND FUTURE CLASS PRESIDENT—

roar!

There was also a small, neat cube of Swiss cheese hanging from the ribbon.

"I feel like I'm leaving a piece of my heart," Lena whispered.

Maggie and Lena continued, winding through town, leaving the posters on the porches of their classmates.

One poster remained, strapped onto Maggie's backpack as they hurried into school. They had run out of time and didn't want to risk being late, which might have aroused suspicion. "We'll sneak in the back door," said Maggie. "It'll be faster."

"Maybe there will still be daisies!" said Lena with enthusiasm. But the bush had turned brown without a single bloom left.

Maggie pulled up on the doorknob as she always did, prepared to whack the door with her hip to make it swing open on its rusty hinges. The door didn't move. She tried again. "How weird . . ." She bent down to examine the doorknob and its lock. The doorknob was brand-new, the lock shiny and expensive.

"Maggie?" said Lena in a carefully controlled voice. "Is that what I think it is?"

Maggie stood up and followed Lena's frightened gaze. There was a small security camera bolted to the side of the building about fifteen feet off the ground. It was pointed directly at the door.

There's no law against trying to get to school on time! whispered her father fiercely.

"Okay," said Maggie to Lena. "Let's not freak out. We'll just walk away. Like we were late for school—"

"We *are* late for school," hissed Lena.

"You don't have to whisper! It's not recording sound!" Then the two girls broke into a run and hurried to the front of the school.

They made it to B-1 after the first bell had rung, but Mrs. Dornbusch hadn't arrived yet. Kayla was taking attendance. "I won't mark you tardy," she said, smiling, and Maggie knew Kayla was in full campaign mode.

"Give me the poster," whispered Lena.

"No! We should just crumple it up. Throw it out. Get rid of it. Wait! Do you think Shute put security cameras in every classroom?" Maggie began to scan the corners of B-1. For someone who loved technology as much as she did, the thought of a Shute-controlled surveillance system sent shivers up her spine.

"Give me the poster," said Lena calmly. "I believe."

Maggie's hand felt shaky as she handed the poster to Lena. Inside her head, she said, *I believe, too.* Even though she didn't, she wanted to.

Lena carried the rolled-up poster, with its bright red

ribbon and offering of cheese, and laid it carefully on Mrs. Dornbusch's desk. No one noticed. Kayla was busy with attendance; Colt was reading a book; Becky, Grace, Brianna, and Shana were talking about the upcoming game against the Mount Carmel Red Tornadoes, which was expected to be a steamrolling since the Tornadoes had lost every game that season; Max and Tyler were playing keep-away with Chris's sneaker while Stevie and Riley cheered them on; Jenna was looking out the window at a flock of birds migrating south; and Lyle was slowly eating a pencil eraser.

A moment later, Mrs. Dornbusch swept into the room and told Kayla, who was lecturing the sixth graders about something, to "put a sock in it." The students immediately sensed that the Dungeon Dragon was in a "scorched earth" mood, and the volume of chatter in the class dropped by half.

Mrs. Dornbusch looked at the poster on her desk, flipped the card over once, then ripped the red ribbon off with one vicious snap of her wrist. Maggie happened to know that it was the poster declaring that *Everyone deserves a turn AT BAT*, and she was certain Mrs. Dornbusch would understand that the poster was a protest against Principal Shute, a man whom Mrs. Dornbusch despised. Would she join the revolution? Would she be on their side? Would she, at the very least, hang the poster on her wall? Perhaps on the chalkboard directly beneath the number 149, which was the number of days she had left at Oda M?

Mrs. Dornbusch's eyes swept over the poster. Then, with unusual force, she crushed it and dropped it in the trash can next to her desk.

TWENTY-FOUR

LUCKILY FOR THE CANDIDACY OF THE Mouse, the sixth graders who had received the anonymous posters that morning had *not* had the same reaction as Mrs. Dornbusch. The posters were everywhere. They overwhelmed the hallways. Crowded the entrance to the cafeteria. Dominated the gym. It seemed like wherever you turned, there was the Mouse staring back at you with his simple message: *You Matter.*

The other candidates had made posters, too. Colt's was handmade, featuring lightning bolts and planets, with the simple slogan: "Vote for Colt." Kayla's poster was more impressive: it looked like she was running for president of the United States. A real photographer had taken her picture, and the professionally printed slogan at the bottom read, *Go for the Gold!*

Still, most of the sixth-grade students were talking about the Mouse—and the fact that Principal Shute had failed to pin responsibility for the posters on any one particular student. After all, there was no rule against helping a candidate hang posters, even if you had no idea who that candidate was.

Meanwhile, Mr. Platt, delighted by the way the sixth graders were getting involved, had hung a few posters of his own that said, *I bet the Mouse would join the Robotics Club if it could. How about you? Meetings are Tuesdays after school in Room 217. ROAR!* Maggie was sure that no one would attend that afternoon's meeting, but she admired Mr. Platt's never-say-die attitude. He was so sure his Robotics Club would be a great success. Someday.

Maggie was waiting for Lena by the flagpole after school, still thinking about Mr. Platt's indomitable spirit, when Lena grabbed her by the shoulders and spun her around. "Talk about a home run! The posters have only been up for a day, and everyone is talking about them. What a great campaign."

As Maggie turned, she caught sight of Allie and Emily getting into Emily's mother's car. Tuesday was the day they rehearsed with the high school chorus. Maggie watched as her old friends laughed about something, completely unaware that she was watching them.

Unaware that she was even there.

Maggie and Lena started to hike up the hill, and Maggie nodded to Lena's chatter about the campaign posters. Lena took out her camera and began a series of action photos of the tops of her shoes as she walked and talked, but Maggie was lost in thought. Seeing Emily and Allie had gotten her thinking about change: how some things change and some things don't. Ever. The bigger things. Her grandfather's creeping illness. Her mother's unending sadness. The things that really mattered.

"You're quiet," said Lena. "Anything wrong?"

"No," said Maggie. "Just thinking."

They continued for a block in silence, before Lena raised the question of their next challenge: the candidate speech. The speech was absolutely mandatory. No speech, no campaign. Maggie and Lena had been kicking around a few ideas that all involved some pretty expensive equipment, like speakers and wireless transmitters. When they reached Maggie's house, a service truck was pulling away.

"Oh, what's he gone and done now?" asked Maggie in exasperation. There was a rule in the house that Grandpop was not supposed to call any service people until Maggie had taken a first look. She could fix most plumbing problems, a lot of wiring issues, and even some structural weaknesses (a couple of which had been caused by her own explosions in the basement).

But when Maggie and Lena walked into the living room, they found Grandpop grinning as if he had just invented the electric lightbulb.

"I got us that Wi-Fi!" he said. "They just finished installing it. There's waves going all through the house," he said, swishing his hands back and forth as if he could see them. "And that means I can finally see what that Vinnie is up to. Go get that computer of yours, Maggie. Bring it down here and fire it up. I'm going on the internet!"

TWENTY-FIVE

"WHAT ARE YOU GOING TO DO?" asked Lena.

"You go back downstairs and stall him," said Maggie, waiting for her system to boot up. "He'll talk to *you* all day. Have a Moxie together. I need at least five minutes."

"But what are you going to do?"

"I'm going to wipe the page. I'll just disconnect the address. Take it off-line."

"But won't that make him suspicious? That Vinnie's Vintage Auto Parts has suddenly disappeared?"

"He *can't* see that website. If he sees the inventory, he's going to know it's his." By now, Maggie had logged into her ISP and was preparing to remove the home page remotely, but she immediately realized that taking down the home page wouldn't be enough. She would have to take down every page on the site. Her business would be destroyed.

"Wow. It's really a conundrum, isn't it?" asked Lena.

"What?" Maggie was tapping furiously on her keyboard.

```
Are you sure you want to delete the file
        "vinnie_inventory_1971.html"?
This action cannot be undone. The file will
be permanently deleted from the server.
```

Delete.

"A problem that is particularly confusing and difficult, one that perhaps has no correct solution."

"I know what the word means!" *Delete. Delete.* "Stop slowing me down!" Maggie had erased half the files.

"Hey!" shouted Grandpop from downstairs. "What's taking you so long? I could have built the pyramids of Egypt by now!"

"I mean," said Lena, "it's his stuff, right? And you're selling it and using the money."

"It's *junk,*" said Maggie. "The only reason it's worth anything is because I spent hundreds of hours sorting it, cleaning it, fixing it, and putting it up on the internet.

Do you know how much time I invested in Vinnie?"

"Still, it's his junk to begin with."

"Yeah, and it's been sitting in the basement for forty years. At least once a year my mother threatens to hire someone to haul it away."

"But she never does, does she?"

"My mother never 'does' anything." Maggie returned her full attention to the computer screen. Talking with Lena about her mother was pointless. How could someone with a mother as remarkable as Lena's understand what it was like to have a mother like Maggie's?

"You're hard on her," said Lena.

"You don't get it," muttered Maggie. She couldn't explain to Lena—whose mother was mounting a world-class glass exhibition at the Louvre—that Maggie's mom's whole life was made up of nothing but broken bits and pieces of a life that no longer existed. Fragments of the dreams of what might have been.

"C'mon," said Maggie, shutting down. "It'll take two of us to carry this thing downstairs." Maggie's computer was a bit of a Frankenstein, cobbled together from scrounged parts—but more capable than it looked. It was massive and ugly—but fast.

They set up the computer on the kitchen table, and Grandpop parked his wheelchair directly in front.

Swatting at Maggie's hands every time they approached the keyboard, he kept saying, "No! Let me do it, so I can do it myself next time."

Next time, thought Maggie with a groan. How long was she going to have to keep Vinnie's Vintage Auto Parts down? It was the complete revenue stream for their hacking, and they had a campaign to run.

It took ten minutes just to walk Grandpop through the basics of turning the computer on, maneuvering the mouse, and using a search engine. When he finally clicked on Vinnie's Vintage Auto Parts in the list provided by Google, he received the error message Maggie had known he would:

404 Error—page not found.
The requested URL was not found on this server.

"What does that mean?" Grandpop asked, pointing a stubby finger at the screen.

"It happens all the time," said Maggie, rotating the screen away from him. "It just means the website is down. We can try again later. Sometimes websites disappear, you know, and they never come back."

"But why?"

"Grandpop, that's just the internet," said Maggie

impatiently. She wasn't about to try to explain the entire modern world to her grandfather, who practically hadn't left the house since Grandmom died a decade ago.

"Was there something in particular you were looking for?" Lena asked softly. "A part?"

"No," mumbled Grandpop, wheeling away. "I just thought it would be nice to . . . you know, talk to someone who knew something about muscle cars. The guts of them. No one seems to care anymore." He disappeared into the kitchen.

"That was so sad," said Lena in a whisper.

"That was *lucky*," said Maggie, shutting down the computer and disconnecting the power cord. Then she caught herself and looked toward the kitchen, where she could hear her grandfather opening and closing the refrigerator. "Yeah, it was kind of sad," she said quietly. "Maybe I can show him how email works. I bet there are lots of people besides 'Vinnie' who are into auto parts for muscle cars." She thought about how small the house felt to her, and how it must feel even smaller to Grandpop, who only ever left it to go to the health clinic once a week, where he was poked and prodded and scolded about the sugary foods he craved.

You can't save him, said her father.

"No, but I can set him up with an email address,"

said Maggie testily.

"I'm not arguing!" said Lena. "See if 'gpops17820@ gmail.com' is taken."

They struggled upstairs with the bulky computer and set it on Maggie's desk, then Maggie threw herself backward on her bed. "You do know that without money coming in, we're dead in the water. Today is Tuesday. The candidate speech is on Monday, less than a week away. What are we going to do with Vinnie's Vintage Auto Parts shut down?"

"Improvise!" said Lena, throwing herself on the bed alongside Maggie and poking her in the ribs with her elbow. "It's what we do best. We're a couple of wing nuts!"

TWENTY-SIX

THE MORNING OF THE CANDIDATE SPEECHES, it poured. Not sprinkled. Not drizzled. Not rained. *Poured.* Great drenching buckets of water dumped out of the sky, and winds of up to forty miles an hour gusted out of the northeast. Every single sixth grader sitting in the cold, dark, moldering auditorium was damp and uncomfortable. Trash cans had been placed throughout the cavernous space to catch the drips that leaked through the ceiling. Lyle had taken off his shoes and was wringing out his socks.

Nine candidates sat on the stage, in various states of nervousness. The three boys wore ties. The six girls wore skirts. There was one chair conspicuously empty—the one that was supposed to be for the Mouse.

The members of the Election Board were also seated on the stage: Mrs. Dornbusch sat with her legs casually crossed, picking the top layer of dead skin off a callus on her hand. Mr. Platt sat next to her and seemed unusually excited. In his hands, he held a video game controller. Maggie and Lena, both wearing skirts as required, were seated next to Mr. Platt. (The night before, Lena had threatened to wear pants and a tie as a protest against outdated dress codes, but Maggie had convinced her to fight one battle at a time.)

Mr. Shute stood at the podium, shuffling his index cards, glaring at the assembled sixth grade, and checking the space above his head to make sure nothing was positioned to fall on him. It was clear that the principal wanted to get through the morning's assembly as quickly as possible. He had placed a strict time limit of three minutes for each speech, which hardly gave anyone a chance to say more than, *My name is _____. Please vote for me.*

Stevie Jencks was the first to the podium, and he announced that he was in favor of a longer lunch period and more early release days. Amy Flitt said that if she were elected class president she would start a committee that would decorate the cafeteria each month with a new theme to "spice things up." And if elected, Stephanie Himmelberger promised to find a way to bring back recess for the sixth graders. All the candidates received applause, though Tyler Grady definitely got the most when he suggested that as class president he would remove all vegetables from the school lunch menu and personally make sure that chicken potpie was never served again.

Mr. Shute tapped his note cards against the podium. There were only two candidates left—Colt DuPrey and Kayla Gold—and Maggie knew the principal could hardly wait to remind everyone that any candidate who did not deliver a speech today would *not* be included on the ballot.

"Next up, Colt DuPrey," said Mr. Shute tersely.

Colt walked slowly to the podium as if it was the dentist's chair. He wasted the first ten seconds of his time by clearing his throat, tugging on the knot of his tie, and looking at his note cards. Maggie worried he was going to pass out, but when he did begin to speak, his voice was quiet and steady.

"My name is Colt DuPrey, and I think I'd make a good class president. Here is why. I'm a good listener. A really good listener. You'd be surprised at all the things I've heard." There was a tiny ripple of laughter. Some of the sixth graders might have been nervous, wondering what conversations they had whispered within earshot of the quiet boy with ears like satellite dishes.

"Why is it important for a class president to listen? Because the president is supposed to represent the people. So I'm not going to stand up here and tell you what I think you want to hear. Instead, I think you should tell me what *you* want. I'll listen. I promise."

He gathered his note cards and took a step away from the podium, but then stopped and turned back. "Mr. Shute, I still have time, don't I?" Mr. Shute held up two fingers to indicate the number of minutes remaining, so Colt returned to the microphone and said, "I might as well say this other thing. Here goes." He took a deep breath in and let it out. "I never in a million years thought I could run for class president. Only popular kids do that, and I'm not popular. I don't like to give speeches. I don't even like to talk." There was more laughter from his classmates, and Colt laughed, too. "I like to read. And I've been reading these books where ordinary kids do incredible things. And then some incredible things started happening at Oda M, and I figured, hey, if a mouse could stuff two hundred tennis balls in a locker, maybe I could at least run for class president. Because what's the worst that can happen? That's my new slogan. 'Colt DuPrey. What's the worst that can happen?' I just came up with that now."

The students clapped loudly and stamped their feet

when Colt walked back to his seat on the stage.

"That's enough!" shouted Mr. Shute.

Lena whispered fiercely in Maggie's ear, "You see what I mean? Do I know how to pick 'em, or what?" But Maggie still wasn't sure. Why would Colt do something to jeopardize his own candidacy?

Mr. Shute stepped up to the podium and leaned in to the microphone. "We have just one more candidate's speech this morning, since it appears that one of our candidates has not shown up." He stared pointedly at the empty chair that was meant for the Mouse. "And so now, here is our current class president, Kayla Gold."

Kayla stood up confidently and strode across the stage. She positioned her note cards carefully in front of her, adjusted the microphone, then flashed her star-tlingly white teeth at the assembled students. Maggie wondered if she'd had her teeth whitened over the weekend at the same time that she'd gone to Wilkes-Barre for an updated haircut and a new outfit.

"Thank you, Principal Shute. Teachers, my fellow classmates and Wildcats. Before I begin my speech, I'd like us *all* to show our class spirit with our special Wildcats cheer!"

As if on cue, everyone in the auditorium chanted, "Huh, huh, huh, huh, ME-OW," and slashed the air with their claws. Even the teachers joined in, except for Mrs. Dornbusch, who was staring off to the side of the stage as if she'd just noticed something rather frightening.

"Spirit!" said Kayla, turning her megawatt smile on the audience. "That's what Oda M is all about. And that's what a vote for Kayla Gold means: you've got SPIRIT! We have a great school, with the best high school football team in the division! How many of you watched our Wildcats beat the Red Tornadoes 55–13 on Friday?" The sixth graders burst into cheering that ate up almost thirty seconds of Kayla's three-minute time slot. *Pretty smart, Kayla,* thought Maggie. *Everybody loves the Wildcats, and everybody loves to win.*

"Listen up!" said Kayla joyfully. "The Wildcats are going to go *all the way* this year." There was more cheering and stamping of feet from the students. "There isn't a team out there that can stop us!" The sixth graders started to stomp the Wildcat Beat, which was a complicated and precise series of knee slaps, foot stamps, and hand claps.

"So here's what I say. Let's support our Wildcats as they cross the finish line for an undefeated season! As your class president, I will make sure we have a school-wide pep rally this Friday—HALLOWEEN—before our Wildcats play their final game of the season.

Winning won't be easy, because we're facing the Danville Ironmen, and our Wildcats will need all the help they can get. But with *our* support and *our* Wildcats spirit, I know our team will win!" The crowd erupted in applause.

"And when we win the Class AA trophy, my father has agreed to treat the entire sixth grade to ice cream and waffles at Edith's Kitchen on the Sunday after the game. It will be a way to celebrate what makes us so *special* and encourage us to be our very best! So show your spirit, and tomorrow on Election Day, GO FOR THE GOLD!" Kayla raised her fist in the air in a way that said, *You know you love me, now go out and vote for me!*

"How does she do it?" Lena whispered to Maggie, just loudly enough to be heard over the hooting, stamping, and hollering of the sixth grade.

"The girl's got charisma," said Maggie, shaking her head in grudging admiration. "And a certain semi-evil knowledge of how to make people do exactly what she wants. What can I say? She's Odawahaka's Taylor Swift."

"Poor Jenna has to follow *that*," said Lena.

Both girls looked at Jenna Mack, who was sitting with her head bent forward, almost touching her knees. "We shouldn't have done this to her," said Maggie. "It isn't fair."

"Fairness doesn't exist. This is middle school."

"When did *you* become a cynic?" asked Maggie, genuinely surprised.

"Ever since I decided *I want to win*," said Lena with a fierceness that Maggie had never heard from her before.

Well, what do you know? said her father. *She's a hacker after all.*

"All right. Settle down," said Mr. Shute, taking his place behind the podium. "A fine speech, Kayla. I like the positive spirit you bring to our school. And that concludes our Candidate Speech Assembly. If you would all return now—"

"Excuse me, Principal Shute!" said Mr. Platt, jumping up from his seat like a prairie dog popping out of his hole. "I have a bit of a, *hmm*, surprise. Something I'd like to share with the sixth grade. And I believe we have time. Since we're one candidate short?"

"Mr. Platt!" Principal Shute said with exasperation. "Assemblies are carefully planned. Carefully timed. If you wanted to make an announcement, you should have cleared it with me yesterday."

"But I only finished it this morning, and quite frankly, I wasn't sure I could make it work." He turned to Mrs. Dornbusch and said confidentially, "Issues with weight distribution and the drive train. I had the wrong coefficient of friction, which created *madness* in my calculations. And then transporting it in this rain—it's a miracle I got it here at all!"

"Settle down, Paul," she said drily. "You might spontaneously combust."

"I might!" he responded gleefully. "I just might." And then he turned to address the sixth graders, completely bypassing the microphone, which Principal Shute had covered with his hand as if he could mute his overenthusiastic math teacher with one weak tactic.

"My friends! As you all know, I have been wanting to kick off a Robotics Club here at Oda M. I was president of the Robotics Club at my middle school *and* high school, and not only did we build some pretty incredible machines, we also won a couple of championships. Now, I'm all in favor of cheering on the football team— Go Wildcats!—but there's no reason the Wildcats have to be the only winning team here at Oda M. Why not have a trophy-winning Robotics Club? So! To give you an idea of what can be done with simple robotics these days, I put together a little demonstration in the hopes that it might encourage a few of you to sign up for the club. Behold!"

He held up the video game controller and pointed it to the left wing of the stage. There was a whirring sound and a clicking noise, as if a swarm of locusts had settled into a nearby tree.

Suddenly, a six-foot-tall mouse made of Legos, K'NEX, Magformers, and Techno Gears rolled into view, paused, turned smoothly to its right, and headed for the podium.

"Wow!" said Lena. "The Mouse showed up!"

Maggie stared in amazement. "Didn't see that coming," she said under her breath.

"The Mouse is in the house!" shouted Max, bouncing out of his seat and throwing both hands over his head. All the sixth graders jumped up, crowding the foot of the stage. All except for Jenna, who remained in her chair, holding on to her stomach.

Mr. Shute, however, threw out his arms, guarding the podium as if it were the Alamo. "Students! Return to your seats. Mr. Platt! Stand down! I order you to stand that mouse down!"

Maggie couldn't take her eyes off the robot. There were so many things she wanted to know. What was the drive train? Was there more than one? Did the robot run on batteries? Where was the battery pack? How much did it weigh? And what else could it do?

"Mr. Platt!" she said. "That is so cool!"

"You want a turn?" he asked. "After all, you . . ." He

pointed at the mouse, winked, and handed her the controller.

"Thanks," she said. She had an intuition when it came to controls of all kinds. She positioned the enormous rodent directly in front of Mr. Shute, and then pressed Button C. The mouse extended its skeletal arm as if to shake hands with the furious principal.

"Does it talk?" she asked Mr. Platt.

"No, sorry. Not enough time." He was smiling from ear to ear.

"That's okay," said Maggie. "We've got that part covered."

During all the commotion, Jenna Mack had quietly climbed the steps on the far left of the stage. "Excuse me, Mr. Shute?" she said, approaching him from behind.

Mr. Shute whirled around as if fearing an attack from the rear, but then quickly whipped back to face the mouse. It was clear that in the battle of the two, he was more afraid of the mouse than he was of Jenna Mack.

"I've been asked to speak on behalf of the Mouse." Jenna's voice was, as always, *mousy*. Mr. Shute ignored her.

Lena hurried over to the podium. "I'm just going to take a couple of pictures for the bulletin board, okay?" She snapped three quick photographs of the principal with the mouse. "And then if I could just get a few of Jenna while she talks."

"She's not a candidate!" insisted Mr. Shute.

"I know I'm not," said Jenna. "But I'm supposed to speak for the Mouse. I have a written paragraph. Mine is labeled 'Number One,' so I think I'm supposed to go first."

"Let me just . . . you know, for the lighting . . ." Lena arranged Jenna behind the podium, adjusting the microphone so that her quiet voice would be heard loud and clear.

"To your seats, students," called out Mr. Platt cheerfully. "We have another speech. What a great day!"

The sixth graders were curious enough to see what the Mouse had to say that they sat back down. Maggie positioned the robotic mouse directly next to Jenna so that it seemed as if the Mouse was truly speaking.

Jenna looked down at her note card, unable to meet the gaze of her classmates. She began to read:

My fellow Oda Mice. I have lived in the walls of this school for many years, and I have watched as many changes have taken place. Our numbers have grown smaller, our town has grown poorer, and after this year, Oda M will be no more. But most distressing of all is that we ourselves have become so accustomed to creeping about, silent when we might be heard, hidden when we might be seen, living our lives in the dark. We accept things the way they are. We have lost hope that tomorrow could be better than today. George Bernard Shaw once said, "You see things; and you say 'Why?' But I dream things that never were; and I say, 'Why not?'"

Jenna sneaked a peek at her classmates, who were all sitting quietly. "Why not?" she repeated. Then she stepped away from the microphone, and her voice was surprisingly strong, even without amplification. "That's where it ends. But I think there might be more?" She scanned the audience.

Lyle stood up, holding a white index card—which had a small corner nibbled away. "Mine says 'Number Two,' so I guess that's me."

"Mr. Whittaker!" Mr. Shute took a step forward. "You are not wearing assembly attire. No tie, no speech."

"Here, dude," said Tyler, who was still up onstage with the other candidates. "Mine's a clip-on!" and he quickly ripped off his own tie and lobbed it across the stage. Lyle managed to hook the clip-on tie over the neckline of his T-shirt.

"We're good?" asked Lyle. "Rules is rules, right, Mr. S? Okay, Number Two. The Mouse speaks!" Lyle looked closely at the index card. "Right. Okay. 'Why not?' That's what the Mouse asked us."

Then his voice became very serious and he read aloud:

> Why not have a student council instead of just one class president so that more students can be involved in running our school? Why not let the students make some real decisions, like who they sit with at lunch? Why not at least keep the library unlocked, trusting that kids won't steal the books? Why not?

Lyle looked up. "That's it. It just stops there. Anyone else?"

Everyone in the auditorium looked around. Would someone else step forward? Or had the Mouse fallen silent?

Colt broke from the line of other candidates and moved toward the podium. "I've got the third card," he said, holding it up. "And I've got a tie, so I guess I'm allowed to speak." He looked at Mr. Shute with just the slightest cock of his head.

"A candidate cannot deliver a speech for another candidate!" insisted Mr. Shute. "That would be absurd."

"Principal Shute," said Mr. Platt with grave deference in his voice. "We have a six-foot-tall robotic mouse on stage. I believe we've already crossed that line."

"It's super short," said Colt, moving to the podium with more confidence than he had shown for his own speech. Without waiting for Mr. Shute's go-ahead, he launched in:

Students of Oda M: A vote for the Mouse is a vote for each and every one of us. Because we all have a responsibility. We all need to be involved. We all need to ensure that government of the mice, by the mice, and for the mice shall not perish from the earth.

Maggie pressed two buttons on the controller, and the robotic mouse lifted both arms in the sign of victory. Lena said, "Oh! It's poetry in motion!" The sixth graders went wild, cheering and stomping and high-fiving each other. Mr. Shute stared at the rebellious mob and, in perhaps the wisest move of his administration, exited backstage.

TWENTY-SEVEN

ELECTION DAY BEGAN WITH AN ARGUMENT. Actually, it began with voting, immediately followed by an argument.

First thing in the morning, all the students placed their votes safely inside the official, locked ballot box. But then the question was: Who would guard the box until the counting took place at lunch? The members of the Election Board had various suggestions, and they were "discussing" them in the conference room.

Mr. Platt suggested that the person who held the key to the ballot box (Mr. Shute) should not be the one to retain possession of the box during those few critical hours.

"Are you saying I can't be trusted?" shouted Mr. Shute. The entire Election Board was crowded into the small conference room, and Mr. Shute fired his words across the table as though they were missiles that could blow Mr. Platt to bits.

"I'm saying," Mr. Platt responded evenly, "that the *perception* of an election can be as important as the *results* of an election. And where this particular election has been somewhat—irregular—it would be wise to go the extra distance and remove any whiff of impropriety."

"Whiff?" Mr. Shute asked menacingly. "Are you saying I *smell?*"

"Oh, for the love of Christmas," said Mrs. Dornbusch, standing up abruptly. She had been playing Super Stickman Golf on her iPhone for the past ten minutes. Reaching across the table, she grabbed the box and headed for the door. "I'll keep it. The rest of you are a bunch of—eleven-letter word that means cave dweller, plural. You can't be trusted with a dull stick."

Mr. Shute smacked the conference table with his copy of the election handbook. "Mrs. Dornbusch, put that box down. You have no authority, no mandate, no standing—"

"That's exactly the point!" she countered. "I'm the only one in this room who doesn't give a lick who wins this election. *I. Don't. Care.* Which makes me the perfect member of this *ridiculous* Election Board to guard the box."

She continued to the door, but Mr. Shute blocked the exit. "You are not leaving with that box!" he said resolutely.

Uh-oh, here it comes, thought Maggie. Her calculations from the first day of school were about to be put to the test. Newton's second law of motion (force equals mass times acceleration). Mrs. Dornbusch was about to be obliterated. Right before their eyes!

The B-1 Bomber stood toe-to-toe with Principal Shute and drew herself up to her full height, staring down at him as if he were a flea. "Listen to me, you spineless bully," she hissed. "I have arthritis, osteoporosis, poor circulation, and a heart murmur. If you don't move out of my way this instant, I'll claim injuries that haven't even been named yet and sue you from here until Judgment Day. Now step aside!" And she swept out of the room with the ballot box under her arm.

Mr. Platt wriggled out of his chair, avoiding Mr. Shute's eyes. "I suppose this meeting is adjourned," he said.

Mr. Shute stood tapping the *Official Odawahaka Middle School Handbook for Student Elections* against the table. His eyes narrowed. He stared hard at Maggie. She felt like his eyeballs were actually cutting into her skin.

"This isn't over," he said. "This has just begun." Then

he marched out of the conference room.

Maggie exhaled. She had been holding her breath without even realizing it.

Mr. Platt shook the change in his pocket. "I should probably start looking for another job," he murmured, staring at the door as if he thought one might be waiting for him around the corner.

"Oh, Mr. Platt," said Lena sorrowfully.

Maggie felt awful. "The robot mouse was incredible," she said, trying to console their math teacher.

Mr. Platt smiled. "Yes. Yes, it was. And we'll always remember that, right? In dark days, in difficult times, we'll remember what we made, what we *built*, with our hands and our hearts, and we'll take pride in that. Because no one can take that away from us." He smiled again, but seemed lost in thought. Then he whispered, "Troglodytes. An eleven-letter word for cave dweller, plural." He shook his head ruefully. "It was fun." They could hear his footsteps fade away in the empty and echoey corridor.

"Ugh!" shouted Maggie. "Now what? The Barn Stormer has the ballot box. Mr. Shute has the key *and* looks like he's plotting to murder someone—quite possibly me. We're both on surveillance tape, and our only source of revenue has been shut down permanently. *And*

Mr. Platt is going to get fired, thanks to us." She was pacing the length of the conference room, but Lena was surprisingly still.

"Not exactly what we'd planned, is it?" said Lena. She looked thoughtful, but not terribly disturbed.

"Lena!" said Maggie in a panic. "The Mouse is going to win! It's going to win the election. What are we going to do then?"

Lena took a deep breath in and let it out slowly. "I don't know. But *not* knowing something is *not* the worst thing on earth, Maggie, despite what your scientist brain tells you. We'll figure it out. And we'll do it together."

During lunchtime, Maggie and Lena were ushered into the conference room by Mrs. McDermott. No one else from the Election Board was there. Both girls carried cafeteria trays of Chicken 'n' Waffles with mashed potatoes and broccoli. The waffles were already soggy.

"How bad do you think this is going to be?" asked Maggie.

"From the smell of it, pretty bad," said Lena.

"No, I mean the meeting, not the food."

"Oh," said Lena grimly. "I brought my camera—to photograph the bodies as they're carried out."

Before either of them sat down, the other three

members entered: Mrs. Dornbusch and Mr. Platt, followed by Principal Shute. It was obvious that they had already been meeting, perhaps in Mr. Shute's office, and that not one of them was happy with the way the meeting had gone. Mrs. Dornbusch carried the ballot box.

"Give me that," said Mr. Shute, holding out his hand to Lena. Confused, she pushed the tray of food over to the principal.

"No! Not that. Your camera."

"N-o-o-o," she said slowly. "It's my camera."

"I won't have any photographs taken. Give it to me now." Maggie knew that he might just as well have asked Lena to tear out her heart and hand it to him. "This nonsense has gone on long enough."

"Why don't I hold it for you, Lena?" said Mr. Platt kindly. "I'll just keep it right here, on the table, where you can see it."

"You will not!" said Mr. Shute. He moved toward Lena but was blocked by several chairs that were in his way. Lena shrank away from him, moving toward the far end of the table.

Mrs. Dornbusch leaned over to Lena and whispered in a growl, "A famous guy once said, 'Never wrestle with a pig. You get dirty, and besides, the pig likes it.'" She held out her claw. Lena hesitated, then placed the camera gently in the Dragon's hand.

"Let's get this over with," snarled Mrs. Dornbusch, sliding the official wooden ballot box down the length of the table to Mr. Shute. "I've got an appointment to have my bunions shaved."

There were seventy-one students at Oda M and seventy-one ballots cast. Mr. Shute read each vote aloud, then passed the ballot to Mr. Platt, who confirmed it with a nod of his head. Maggie and Lena recorded each vote on their separate tally sheets. At the end of the tabulation, Maggie and Lena added up the votes, made sure their totals matched, and handed the sheets to Mr. Shute.

There was no controversy about the final results: Kayla received nine votes; Stevie Jencks, Stephanie Himmelberger, and Amy Flitt each received two; and Tyler Grady received four. The Mouse received fifty-two. It was a landslide by any definition of the word.

"So," said Mr. Shute, gathering the ballots together in a neat pile and placing them in the pocket of his coat. "This vote never happened, and anyone who says otherwise will be completely and utterly destroyed." He turned first to Maggie.

"Maggie, I've reached out to the admissions department at MIT. Enough said? The videotape is safely in my possession.

"Lena, I looked into your family's background. It's problematic, wouldn't you say? But perhaps it explains a few—oddities. I'm sure I can count on your cooperation.

"Paul. Make no mistake about it: you have always been expendable. In fact, I already have somebody lined up for your job."

Lena reached over and grabbed Maggie's hand. Maggie wasn't sure whether Lena was asking for support or giving it. In the end, it didn't really matter.

"And Mrs. Dornbusch." Mr. Shute turned to the Barn Stormer, who was leaning back in her chair with both hands clasped comfortably across her stomach. She gave the appearance of being on the verge of dozing off, as if she were watching a fairly dull program on TV, long after midnight.

"Oh, Shout," she said, rousing herself slightly. "Let's not pretend you can threaten me. I'm bulletproof."

"It's true I can't fire you," conceded Mr. Shute. "But make no mistake. I can make your last year at Odawahaka Middle School one *you will never forget.*" He leaned forward, the knuckles of both hands resting on top of the massive conference table. Maggie thought he resembled a gorilla, except that gorillas have an unmistakable look of intelligence in their eyes.

Mrs. Dornbusch allowed her gaze to drift to the

ceiling. "Sometimes I feel as though no one listens to me. I. Don't. Care. Rig the election. I don't care. Fire Paul. I don't care. Send these two to Alcatraz. I don't care." She leaned forward and pressed both palms onto the top of the table. "I have one hundred and forty-four days left in this place, and then I'm buying a twenty-nine-foot cabin cruiser with a three-hundred-and-seventy-five-horse-power inboard motor, and I'm going to spend the rest of my days sailing around the Florida Keys. I'm going to fish. I'm going to swim with dolphins. I'm going to drink piña coladas with pink paper parasols sticking out of them. So do what you want, Shute. I don't *like* you. But I don't care."

Oh. Maggie felt something die inside her. She hadn't even realized how much she'd been hoping that the dragon in Mrs. Dornbusch would rise up and incinerate Mr. Shute. But instead, the fiery Dungeon Dragon had turned out to be nothing more than a piddling stream, seeking the path of least resistance as it made its eventual escape to the sea.

"We are adjourned. File out." Mr. Shute stood to the side of the door and waited as each person walked out of the room.

Maggie hurried ahead of Lena, who retrieved her camera. Both girls carried their cardboard lunch trays, the food untouched and now turned cold. "Don't even start on me," Maggie said as they stepped into the privacy of the stairwell. There was a large trash barrel there, and Maggie threw away her tray, food and all. "I'm not blowing my chance to get into MIT. That's been my dream my whole life, and I'm not throwing it away for a *mouse*."

"I know," said Lena sorrowfully, picking up a cold and soggy waffle before dropping the rest of her lunch in the trash.

"And it wouldn't be fair to Mr. Platt. He needs his job."

"I know, I know. It's just that . . ." Lena nibbled on the edge of the waffle.

"What?" said Maggie, whirling around. "What, exactly? This was just supposed to be fun. Hacking is *fun*. It's a brain challenge. A puzzle. A joke. That's all it was ever supposed to be."

Lena dumped the rest of her waffle in the trash barrel. "Go on! Tell yourself that if you want to," she said angrily. "You know, Maggie, I still can't figure out why you're determined to make yourself *so small*."

She walked away.

At the end of the day, Principal Shute came on the PA system and announced that Kayla Gold had been elected class president.

Maggie didn't say anything to Lena, and Lena didn't say anything to Maggie. They hadn't spoken to each other since lunch.

TWENTY-EIGHT

THAT AFTERNOON, THERE WAS A SHARP knock on Maggie's bedroom door. Maggie, who had been looking through her father's box of memories, shoved the box under her bed and then said, "Come in."

"I need to talk to you," said her mother, walking in and pacing back and forth across the floor several times before her eyes settled on something. Maggie followed her gaze and saw that she was looking at the photograph taped to her computer that Lena had created of Maggie with her father at MIT.

"How did you . . . ?"

"Lena did it with Photoshop," said Maggie. She stared at the picture along with her mother. It was as if they were flies suddenly trapped on the sticky pesticide tape they hung on the porch in the summertime.

"I got a call . . . ," began her mother, peeling her eyes away from the photograph, "from your principal. He claims that he has videotape of you trying to break into the school."

"That's a lie!" said Maggie. "We were just trying to get to school on time."

Maggie's mother waved her hand. "He's got a whole list: Trespassing. Vandalism. Lying to school officials."

"Principal Shute has *issues*, Mom. I seriously think he's delusional. And totally paranoid. He carries this baseball bat with him everywhere he goes, and he spends more time on his cell phone than he does running the school. And . . ." Maggie knew she was running out of ammunition. "And . . . what do you care anyway?"

Maggie's mother rubbed her forehead slowly. "What is that supposed to mean?"

"Really, Mom? When is the last time you came into my room?"

"Oh! Is *that* what we're going to argue about now? *My* parenting skills? Look, I'm the first to admit that I could do better. I know other mothers sew curtains for their daughters' bedrooms and vacuum every day and tidy up their toys, but those aren't the only things that count."

"Well, they count for something," said Maggie.

"That, and maybe not drinking every night."

"I haven't had a drink in three days," her mother said sharply. "In case you haven't noticed, which I'm sure you haven't. Why would you? So busy with your own schemes. Your own plans. Your own dreams. You know, you really are like your father. He—"

Maggie held her breath. Was her mother about to tell her something about her father? She had waited so many years to hear something, anything about him.

There was the sound of a van pulling up in front of the house, and the mechanical sigh of a hydraulic lift lowering itself.

"Your grandfather is home. I'm going out."

"Out where?" asked Maggie. She imagined her mother returning from the liquor store on Route 42 and then hiding in her room.

"A meeting." Maggie's mother had already retrieved her cell phone from her pocket and was speed-dialing a number. Her hands shook, but the call went through.She spoke quietly into the phone before hanging up and then heading for the door. She stopped with one hand on the doorknob.

"Principal Shute said he's one step away from bringing criminal charges. If he does that, you won't be going to MIT. So think, Maggie. Think about what you do next and why. I know it isn't *brilliant* to be cautious. There isn't any genius to being the one who follows the rules. And there's no glory in getting up every day and going to work and then coming home each night. But in the end, ask yourself: who's left standing?" She tapped the photograph on Maggie's computer. "And whether that means anything to you."

Maggie listened as her mother walked out the back door, got in her car, and drove away.

Your mother—, whispered her father.

"Shh," said Maggie quietly. "I'm thinking." She felt her father's annoyance and disapproval. Usually, they were in complete agreement about her mother.

In a minute, Maggie went downstairs and found her grandfather browning ground meat and onions in a heavy skillet, the sizzle and pop of the beef fat seeming to match the dark mood he was in. On the counter, there was an open package of Hamburger Helper.

"I went to the library today!" he announced, scraping the bottom of the pan with a wooden spatula.

"Really?" asked Maggie. "What for?"

"To see if I could find that website I told you about."

"Oh," said Maggie. Vinnie's Vintage Auto Parts had been off-line for a week. She could hardly bear to think of her hard work lost.

"And I learned a few things," said Grandpop. "There was a very helpful librarian—a young gal not much older than you—whose job it is to get old people like me squared away with the internet. She got me an email account!"

"Wow, Grandpop," said Maggie. "That's great." But inside, she was thinking, *Uh-oh. Here comes trouble.*

"Now, do *you* know how to do a search on the internet?" he asked.

"Yes, Grandpop, I do."

"Well, good, because there's really a lot going on in the world outside of this house." He poured water into the skillet, then added the contents of the box. "The librarian was able to find other people who've been asking about Vinnie's Vintage Auto Parts, too. You know, wondering where the website went. Past customers, and such."

Maggie felt like a giant headache was literally landing on top of her head—a Death Star–sized headache brought on by the thought of discussing the internet with her grandfather.

"And they sent me photos of parts they bought from the website." Grandpop turned up the flame beneath the pan to bring the whole thing to a boil. He seemed almost angry at the food on the stove, the way he pushed it around with the spoon. *"Vinnie's Vintage Auto Parts. Can you imagine that? Photographs of the actual parts that have been sold from that website."*

The contents of the skillet had begun to boil, and he turned the heat down to a simmer. "Some of the parts were truly unique. One of a kind. Unforgettable."

The smell of ground meat and onions hung heavily in the small kitchen, and the air between Maggie and her grandfather seemed thick with the weight of the odor and grease.

"I'm sorry, Grandpop," said Maggie.

"You should be," he said, looking her straight in the eye. "You don't rob a man in his own home. And you don't steal from family. Ever. *Family*, Maggie. Family, in the end, is the only thing that matters."

Maggie hung her head. She had been selfish—taking what she wanted and convincing herself it didn't hurt others. And she had been cowardly—afraid to stand up to Principal Shute even though she knew he was wrong.

"I'll pay you back," said Maggie.

"Yes, you will," said Grandpop grimly. "Now off with you. Bed without supper."

Maggie walked slowly upstairs and into the darkness of her room. She lay down on her bed. How had everything come to this? She hadn't meant to hurt Grandpop, but she had. She hadn't meant to give Principal Shute the power to destroy her dreams, but she had. She hadn't meant to drive her mother out of the house—and away from her—but she had.

Come on! Don't lose focus now, said her father. *You've got bigger problems to solve.*

Maggie lay in the quiet of the house—no TV, no clink of ice cubes, no arguing—allowing the bad, dark thoughts to circle in her head. They swirled and swooped, around and around, but never seemed to land anywhere. These weren't the thoughts Maggie liked to have. She liked the straight-line kind of thoughts that marched in order. The ones on the ground that carried her from Point A to Point B.

After a few minutes, a new thought entered her head. *Maybe I should stop taking advice from a dead guy.*

TWENTY-NINE

"WE SHOULD GO TO THE GAME in costume," said Lena the next day as she and Maggie walked home from school. "Don't you think? It would give us something new to work on."

In two days it would be Halloween, a Friday, and the whole town would be at the final football game of the season, when the Odawahaka Wildcats would face off against the Danville Ironmen in the hopes of having their first undefeated season.

When they arrived at Maggie's front gate, Lena gasped and Maggie looked up to see a bizarre sight on the front of her house: There was a knife, long handled and gleaming, stabbed into the metal frame of the front screen door. An envelope was pinned by the blade, and rivers of blood dripped from its shiny metal surface, as if the heart of the house itself had been stabbed and was in the act of dying. Maggie's thoughts jumped to her grandfather. Was he inside? Had he been hurt? Her eyes darted to the driveway. Her mother's car wasn't there.

"There's writing on the envelope," whispered Lena. It was too hard to make out the words from the front gate. The writing was scribbled, written in haste, using a thin ballpoint pen.

"Isn't that one of the envelopes from school?" asked Maggie. "You know, the kind that gets passed around with teachers' names on it?" Maggie and Lena approached the door.

"The blood! It's fake!" said Lena, but Maggie had already figured that out. Even a sharp blade wouldn't go through metal, and besides, the "river" of blood was flapping in the breeze. It was just a ghoulish Halloween decoration—a half knife with a really strong magnet on one end so that it looked like it was plunged into the door. The blood was red, gummy plastic.

"Not a bad hack!" said Maggie, her spirits lifting. Effective, inexpensive, and it didn't leave a trace of damage. She plucked the knife off the door and read the scribbled note on the outside of the envelope: *It's in your hands now. —I.C.*

"Who's I.C.?" asked Lena.

"I don't know," said Maggie, holding the envelope.

"Let's open it in my room."

They hurried through the door, but a voice shouted at them from the back of the house.

"I'm stuck on the toilet!"

"Oh, for Pete's sake!" groaned Maggie. "Grandpop! Just . . . sit tight." Which even she could tell was an unnecessary directive. "I'll be there in a minute." She and her grandfather hadn't spoken since yesterday, and she didn't want to have their first conversation in front of Lena. She turned to her friend. "C'mon. We'll open the envelope in my room and then . . . I'll come down and . . . figure something out with him."

"Maggie," whispered Lena. "We have to help him now."

"He can wait," said Maggie, shaking the envelope urgently.

Grandpop shouted from the bathroom: "I'm not getting any younger!"

"I'll be there in a couple of minutes!" Maggie yelled back. She put her foot on the first step, but Lena rested a hand on her arm.

"Maggie, he's scared," said Lena.

Huh! Right! said her father's voice. *That man doesn't get scared. He just makes life scary for everyone else.*

Maggie paused. She looked at Lena. "You're right," she

said slowly. "This"—she held up the envelope—"can wait."

"Maggie!" barked her grandfather in a hoarse voice. "Get your monkey butt in here!" But the door to the small bathroom wouldn't open. "It's my stinking wheelchair," said Grandpop. "It got wedged under the sink somehow, and now I can't move it. So I can't get *into* the chair, and I can't get the door open to get out."

Maggie pushed against the door, but it opened only an inch. She pushed harder. Her father's voice scolded her: *Brute force is the last resort of the incompetent.* It was one of his favorite sayings, scrawled in several places in his notebooks.

"I'm not incompetent," she muttered.

"No one said you were," whispered Lena. "Just think."

In the end, they got the door off its hinges, though it took some clever maneuvering and a solid understanding of stress points and the application of force at an angle. Maggie's grandfather wrangled himself back into his wheelchair, and the girls pushed him to the couch. Once there, he rolled himself out of the chair—knocking it over—and landed on the sofa like a giant tuna hauled onto the deck of a fishing boat.

Maggie bent down to pick up the wheelchair, but her grandfather said, "Leave it! I hate that chair. I hate it," and he kicked it with his good leg, over and over until one of the wheels fell off.

Maggie didn't know what to say. Grandpop couldn't get around without his wheelchair. That was just a fact of life.

"Grandpop . . ."

"I need rest," he said. "Just leave it, Mags. Leave it and let me rest."

"Okay," said Maggie. Her mother would be home soon. Maybe she would know what to do.

Maggie and Lena walked slowly upstairs, the mysterious envelope in Maggie's hand. "That was sad," whispered Lena once they'd closed the door to Maggie's bedroom.

Maggie didn't want to talk about it. She wasn't used to seeing her grandfather this way. It was easier to deal with his usual snarl and bark. Maybe that was why he was so demanding and difficult. It made it easier for her, easier than seeing him sad and sick.

The envelope called to her.

Maggie dumped the contents onto her bed: a pile of papers that looked like the votes that had been cast in yesterday's election. Maggie and Lena began to sift through them, trying to make sense of what they were looking at.

"They could be fakes," said Maggie.

"They're not fakes," said Lena.

"But they're photocopies," pointed out Maggie, as if this might be a reason to doubt them. Seventy-one of them.

"You look for yours," said Lena. "I'll look for mine." The girls split the pile in half, each flipping through page after page.

"Here's mine," said Lena, holding up one of the photocopies. "I know because I started to write a checkmark, then changed it to an X."

"Here's mine." It was easy to spot. Maggie had marked her ballot with a small mouse paw print in the lower left corner.

They were holding proof that the Mouse had won the election for class president. Or were they?

"Who did this?" asked Maggie suspiciously. "Who photocopied the ballots?"

"Maybe Shute did it."

"No. He wouldn't stick them to my door. Who's 'I.C.'?"

"Okay. Names that begin with the letter *I*," said Lena. "Irene?"

"Isabel?"

"Ivy?"

A memory from the first day of school popped into

Maggie's head. *Not Mary. Not Molly. Not Martha* . . . "It's not a name!" shouted Maggie. "It's an avowal."

"A vowel?"

"No! An avowal. A confession. It's a battle cry!"

Maggie poked each letter on the envelope. "I. Care." She looked at Lena and smiled. "She cares! She actually cares!"

"I knew it!" shouted Lena, her long legs shooting out from under her as she jumped to her feet. "I knew it all along. Under those baggy sweatshirts, behind those frozen eyes—she cares!" Lena started to whirl and lift her arms up to the sky, as though she'd been praying for rain through a long, hot drought and the deluge had finally arrived.

The Dungeon Dragon. The Queen of the Count-down. The woman who claimed she couldn't remember Maggie's name but somehow knew where she lived.

"Wait!" said Maggie. She reached out and grabbed hold of Lena's arm, halting her in mid-twirl. "The note says, 'It's in your hands now.'"

"Yes!" said Lena, holding up a handful of the papers. "The proof is in our hands now."

"But what are we going to do with it? We need to think this through. There are so many ways this could go wrong."

"We show the ballots to someone."

"Mr. Shute would say they're fake. He would say the real ballots were thrown out. Trashed. Or maybe he even made fake ballots, in case anyone asked to see? It wouldn't be hard to do. Anyone could make fake ballots."

"But we know these are ours. We remember our own ballots," said Lena.

"So we need to get everyone at school to identify a ballot. Same as we did."

"No," said Lena. "The Mouse needs to do it. Because that's what the Mouse is all about. *E pluribus unum.* Out of many, one."

The girls heard the front door open and then close downstairs, followed by, "What . . . *happened?*"

"My mom's home," said Maggie. Her mother did not sound like she'd had a good day. Maggie hoped Lena would leave before her mom started . . .

Lena seemed to understand. "We can figure out the details later," she said. "Give me the ballots. I've got some scanning to do."

When Maggie and Lena arrived at Oda M the next morning, they both noticed that Principal Shute's reserved parking space was empty. Lena carried the poster she'd made, and Maggie, of course, had extra-strength double-sided tape. They weren't going to ask anyone else to handle this task. They would do it on their own. No sneaking around. They had come out of the walls for good.

They hung the poster on the wall right next to the main office so that any student who walked in the front door would see it. It didn't take long before a crowd of students had gathered around.

"That one's mine," said Emily. She nodded at Allie, who had already found her ballot.

"There's mine," said Becky.

"I don't see mine," said Tyler, worried. He kept scanning the poster. "Oh, there it is!"

The poster was simple: all seventy-one ballots displayed in neat rows. Anonymous. Complete. *Authentic.* Every student could identify his or her own ballot, even if some didn't declare ownership out loud. For those who chose to remain silent, the message was the same: the ballots were real because each person could see that his or her ballot was real.

"Nine!" said Kayla. "Nine votes! What is wrong with you people?"

"It's actually not bad," said Lyle philosophically. "You were the first runner-up."

"I lost to a rodent!" she shouted. Her face turned

bright red, something that Maggie had never seen happen to Kayla in all the years she'd known her. Kayla walked stiffly in the direction of the girls' bathroom. Maggie felt bad for her. Truly bad. The first bell would ring in a minute, but it looked like Kayla would be in the bathroom for a while.

"Incoming," warned Max, facing the front door.

Maggie turned to see Principal Shute standing in the doorway, his briefcase in one hand and his baseball bat in the other. He surveyed the assembled sixth-grade class, then his eyes rested on the poster.

"Mrs. McDermott," shouted Mr. Shute. "Make an announcement. Immediately. Every student and teacher is to report to the auditorium at once. No one is excused for any reason." He then tucked his bat under his arm, marched forward, and ripped the poster down the middle, leaving just the edges, like broken limbs, hanging from the wall. "All of you. Fall in. Single file. March!"

The students did as they were told, but was it Maggie's imagination or was there a hint of defiance in the way they walked? They entered the auditorium and sat down in the first few rows of seats. Only the aisle lights were turned on, the ones that glowed with a pinprick of yellow light to prevent anyone from tripping once a show had begun. Otherwise, the enormous room was dark, the stage empty, the soaring ceiling swallowed up in blackness.

Mr. Shute stood on the floor in front of the seated students, holding his bat at his side. He stared ahead, ramrod straight, and waited. No one made a sound.

Usually, during assemblies, the teachers joined the principal on stage. But today, Principal Shute was on the ground, and as each teacher entered the auditorium one by one, they sat with the students. Mr. Platt smiled at the sixth graders as if to say, *It's not so bad!* Mrs. Matlaw looked at the students fiercely, letting them know that she would throw herself on a live grenade to protect each and every one of them if she had to. Mr. Esposito sat still, not even fussing with his tie, and Mr. Peebles simply seemed confused.

Mr. Shute continued to wait. Maggie counted the students. Seventy. The only one missing was Kayla. Chances were that she hadn't even heard the announcement, and if she had, she was in no condition to face her classmates.

There was one conspicuous absence. Mrs. Dornbusch.

A low murmur began, a whispering sound that was like leaves on a dry night. *The Mouse is in the house. The Mouse is in the house.* It was so quiet, you could hardly make out the words.

Mr. Shute lifted his baseball bat and let it fall with a thunderous crack that echoed throughout the giant auditorium.

"This will end *now!*" he announced. "I have been too lenient. Too forgiving. Too lax. And this is the result. Breaking ranks. Disobeying orders. *Treason.*" He hissed the last word as if it were a serpent that slithered at their very feet.

"I am going to ask one question, and I am going to receive an instant answer. *Who is the Mouse?* Step forward now! And if there is a conspiracy of students—*a rats' nest*—trust me when I say that I will dig out each and every one of you."

The sixth graders sat still. Maggie felt her breath catch in her throat, and she leaned slightly to the left so that her shoulder was touching Lena's. Lena laid a hand on Maggie's.

Mr. Shute stared at the sixth-grade class. His voice was quiet. "If the misbehaving student does not step forward within the next fifteen seconds, you will *all* remain after school today for one hour's detention."

No one moved. Maggie tried again to breathe, but it was as if someone had placed a heavy hand on her chest.

"Very well," said Mr. Shute. "If someone does not

step forward in the next fifteen seconds, you will all face detention *and* I will suspend all school social activities from now through the end of the year."

There was a murmur of dismay from the students, but still no one stepped forward. Maggie wondered if the other students really didn't know, or were they simply protecting their own?

Lyle shifted in his seat. Jenna bowed her head. Max and Tyler were still.

A slow and sticky grin spread across Mr. Shute's face, and that was when Maggie realized. It was just as Mrs. Dornbusch had said: *The pig likes it.* Mr. Shute was enjoying himself.

"If the culprit who has disrupted our school and dishonored us all does not step forward in the next *five* seconds, I will use my disciplinary powers, which are far ranging, to forbid each and every one of you from attending tomorrow's final football game of the season."

The sixth graders gasped. To miss the game, to miss the chance to see the Wildcats—their no-name team from their no-name school in their no-name town—win the final game in an undefeated season, something that had never happened in the history of Odawahaka, was more than they could bear. It was as if Mr. Shute had announced that they would all face a firing squad at dawn.

Maggie knew: it wasn't fair to them. She slid forward, planting her feet on the hard floor, and wondered if her legs would hold her up.

"*Mus, sum!*" announced a voice from the darkened aisle. All the sixth graders turned in their seats toward the back of the auditorium. Kayla marched forward, confident and determined. A born leader. Even in the dim light, Maggie could see that she'd been crying—and crying hard—but her face was composed now. "*Mus, sum,* Mr. Shute. I am the Mouse. Which means"—she glanced triumphantly at the other students—"I *won* the election!"

Mr. Shute was stunned into silence, but Maggie was fit to be tied. How *dare* she? How dare Kayla take credit for all of Maggie and Lena's hard work? Kayla Gold engineering the Opera Mouse? Kayla Gold executing the Epic Balls-on-Shute Hack? Kayla Gold creating the chemical compound of nitrogen triiodide and transferring it safely to the gym without blowing her eyebrows off? It was absurd. It was beyond belief. It was more than Maggie could bear.

"*Mus, SUM!*" she said, standing up and hurling the words at Kayla.

But Lyle was already on his feet. "Actually, Mr. Shute. *Mus, sum.*" He waved sheepishly, as if he'd just admitted to farting.

266

"No," said Jenna, shaking her head gravely. *"Mus, sum."*

"Yeah, me too," said Max. *"Mus, sum.* Right, Ty?" He nudged Tyler with his elbow. *"Mus, sum* for you, too."

Colt stood up next, with Lena bringing up the rear, at which point every student from Table 10 had declared himself or herself to be the Mouse.

But then Allie and Emily stood up together and declared in unison, *"Mus, sum!"* They smiled at Maggie, and Emily gave her a wink.

And then the other sixth graders joined in, until nearly all of them were on their feet, insisting, *"Mus, sum."*

"What are they *doing*?" asked Mr. Shute.

Mr. Esposito practically floated out of his seat. "They're speaking *Latin. Latin!"* He put both hands to his heart as though he feared it might burst from his chest. "Oh, most beautiful tongue. The language of Virgil and Cicero and Caesar." Then he raised both hands above his head and exclaimed, *"Mus, sum! Ubi concordia, ibi victoria!"* Mr. Esposito must have been confident that Mr. Shute wouldn't know the meaning of *that* Latin phrase: "Where there is unity, there is victory."

Out of the corner of her eye, Maggie saw the stage curtain ripple and a smudge of gray dissolve back into the shadows.

Mrs. Dorn-Mouse.

I guess it's never too late to earn a new nickname, thought Maggie.

The class had taken up the familiar chant, "The Mouse is in the house! The Mouse is in the house!" and Maggie joined in, arms linked with Lena.

The Mouse is in the house!

It was the first time Maggie had ever enjoyed taking part in a group cheer.

THIRTY

PRINCIPAL SHUTE RESIGNED THAT VERY DAY. The news spread through the town with the speed of electricity running down a copper wire. All along Main Street, the gossip was that he'd been applying for a new job since his first day at Oda M.

"*Semper fidelis!*" scoffed Mrs. Dornbusch in the lunchroom that day. "Some people have no concept of loyalty."

The only thing left was a victory celebration. The Mouse had won the election, and Oda M was free of Principal Shute. "*Hackito, ergo sum gaudium!*" declared Maggie, which even she admitted was a really bad translation: "I hack, therefore I am joyous!" But Lena and Maggie decided to write it into the Hacker's Bible as the Eleventh Commandment anyway. It was the first time Maggie had ever *added* something to her father's notebooks, and it felt right to do it with Lena.

"What's wrong with you?" shouted Grandpop on Friday morning as Maggie dozed at the kitchen table next to her toast.

She and Lena had been up all night preparing the celebration. There was only one place it could be, only one place where the entire town would be gathered, hopefully in victory. But to prepare the hack on such hallowed ground had required real "nightwork." All-night work. Maggie didn't know how she would make it through the day, much less a morning argument with Grandpop.

"Nothing." She sat up and resumed eating her toast. Grandpop wheeled around the kitchen, fixing a bowl of oatmeal. Every time he passed her chair, he knocked into it, and Maggie had a hard time believing it was entirely accidental.

"I've been meaning to ask you," he grumbled. "What did you get for the Chevy gas pedal?"

"The 1959 Impala or the 1953 Bel Air?"

Grandpop looked surprised. "The Impala."

"A hundred and ten, plus shipping. It was in good condition, and there aren't many originals around." Maggie was so tired, her toast kept going in and out of focus in front of her eyes. "I got more for the Bel Air, though. I think one eighty."

Her grandfather stopped his wheelchair right in front of her. "How many pieces have you sold?"

Maggie shrugged. "A hundred, at least. But most of the parts aren't even listed on the website yet. You know, Grandpop, you've got a couple thousand auto parts in that basement."

"So how come you haven't listed 'em?"

"It takes time! To research each one—figure out what year and what car and what part it is."

"Well, for dang's sake," said Grandpop, turning his wheelchair to face the stove, then suddenly wheeling it back around to face her head on. "Just ask *me*. I can tell you every little thing about every part that's down there. Why didn't you come to me in the first place?"

Maggie looked at her grandfather. It was a fair question, but she was too tired to come up with the answer. She took another bite of her toast and rested her head on her arm as she chewed.

"Well, who knew?" murmured Grandpop.

Then he perked up. "Actually, *I* did. I always said it. I told your mother over and over. It's a gold mine down there." He wheeled himself to the refrigerator and poured himself a glass of skim milk. "And *you* figured out how to make it pay. I never would have thought of a website. For pity's sake, I'd never even been on the *internet*."

Maggie smiled. She felt like she was seeing her grandfather in a different way. Or maybe it was just exhaustion.

"So, we'll be partners," said Grandpop. "We'll split the profits fifty-fifty, and you'll pay me back for the parts you already sold. And after *that*, you can save the rest of what you make for that fancy East Coast college you've got your heart set on." He wheeled himself back to the stovetop, where his oatmeal was bubbling and belching. "But I have a secret for you, Maggie Gallagher, and don't you forget it. You think you get all your mechanical genius from your dad? Well, there's a little piece of it that comes from me. I was taking apart and putting together Hemis before your father was even born."

Maggie put the last bite of toast in her mouth and stood up. "Thanks, Grandpop," she said, dropping a kiss on the top of his head. "I won't forget."

When Maggie came home that afternoon, she climbed straight into bed and slept for four hours. Then she hustled to get dressed so she and Lena could catch the six-thirty game bus in front of the Opera House. She noticed on her way down the hall that her mother's bedroom was dark, the door open, and there was no noise of the TV coming from the living room.

Her mother, it turned out, was sitting on the living room couch with her feet in thick wool socks propped up on the coffee table. Next to her was an open can of Moxie. The keys on her laptop made a steady *click-clack, click-clack* that made Maggie think of the train that used to run through Odawahaka, back in the day.

"Where's Grandpop?" asked Maggie.

"Out," said her mother. "He seems to be getting out more than he used to. Have you noticed?" She turned around, smiling, and looked at Maggie. Then the smile faded from her face, and she said, "Huh. Look at you."

"What do you mean?"

Her mother looked at her closely. "You look like you're dressed for nightwork." And there was a wistful sound in her voice. Then she laughed. "I can see a nine-volt battery peeking out from under your Wildcats hat. And that bulge under your coat isn't from a jack-o'-lantern."

Maggie shifted the tool kit under her coat and stuffed her hair more carefully under the hat.

"Better?"

"Better."

"Are you going to the game?" Maggie tried to make the question sound casual.

"No." Maggie's mother smiled. "It's . . . hard . . . for me to be back, sometimes. You know, to run into people I knew in high school." She grew quiet. "Sometimes I think that people from the town are disappointed in me. I was . . . well, I was supposed to be the Golden Girl. It sounds so funny to say it now. As if it even means anything. But I was supposed to become something they could be proud of, 'hometown girl makes good,' you know? That sort of thing. But I ended up right back here." She looked around the living room as if seeing it for the first time. "And then other times I think they've just"—she hitched her shoulders up once and let them drop—"forgotten all about me, like the girl I was never even existed." She examined the can of Moxie in her hand. "Neither feeling is great."

"Mom?" Maggie advanced into the room and sat on one arm of the couch. "Why *did* you come back? I mean, I know Dad died, but why didn't you stay in Boston?"

Her mother shook her head slowly as if trying to remember herself. "I didn't have it in me. Your dad was so . . . it's hard to put into words. He was dynamic. Like some brilliant supernova. Next to him, everybody just seemed to fade away. He was the one with all the ideas, all the dreams, all the energy. *I* was the one who kept things running, who held down a regular job, who made sure the bills got paid. And then when he died, I was so . . . shocked . . . and sad. And I was pregnant with you and overwhelmed. I didn't think I could make it on my own. And honestly," she said with a laugh though tears sparkled in her eyes, "I just wanted my mom." She was quiet for a minute. "And then you were born, and Grand-mom died, and I stayed."

Maggie looked down at the floor. "I hate it here," she whispered.

"I know you do," murmured her mother, resting her head against the back of the couch. "But it's a big, bad world out there, Maggiekins. Believe me. It can just swallow you up and spit you out like you're nothing more than a crumb. Home is safe." She clutched the can of Moxie so hard a dent formed on one side. "God, I want a drink." She closed her eyes and took several long, deep breaths in and out.

She opened her eyes. "So when do you think you'll be home?"

"I don't know," said Maggie, standing up. She suddenly felt defensive thinking about the hack that she and Lena were hoping to pull off.

"It's just a question, Maggie," said her mother, sounding hurt. "It's not the Spanish Inquisition. It's the kind of question mothers ask."

But you never do, thought Maggie.

Her mother sighed. "I guess what I'm really asking is, 'Are you going to be safe?'"

Maggie took a deep breath in. "That's the plan."

Her mother nodded, unhappy. "Come here." Maggie moved closer and her mother pushed Maggie's unruly hair under the Wildcats hat so that the battery was more securely hidden. "All Tech Men carry batteries!" said her mother. "Right?" Then she laughed.

Maggie laughed, too. "Yes, we do!" She headed for the door, then turned back and added, "Don't worry, okay?"

"Just be smart," said her mother, putting the can of Moxie on the coffee table and returning both hands to her laptop. Then she laughed again, as if recognizing that "being smart" was actually more of the problem than the solution when it came to Maggie.

THIRTY-ONE

TIMING IS EVERYTHING IN A HACK. In that regard, this one should have been simple. The home field for the Wildcats had a low fence around it and no security system. Maggie and Lena had stayed up all night laying wire, burying a small hydraulic press and a large inflatable mouse under the grass on the football field, and attaching an additional electrical outlet to the sprinkler system fuse box located under the bleachers. All they had to do once the game was over—win or lose—was plug the cord from the hydraulic press into the outlet. The Mouse would inflate midfield, and the celebration would begin. And if the team lost, hopefully the hack would lift everyone's spirits or at least give the fans something to talk about on the bus ride back to the Opera House.

The Wildcats stadium was packed. Of course the

entire town of Odawahaka was there, but the fans from Danville had traveled the short ten miles to fill the visitor stands and cheer for their Ironmen.

"Is it always this crowded for the last game of the season?" asked Lena as she and Maggie squeezed onto the end of a bleacher.

"This is insane," said Maggie. "I've never seen it like this." She wondered if the bleachers were strong enough to hold this many people. Clearly, the stadium was over capacity.

Lena, who knew nothing about football, followed Maggie's lead in cheering and booing at the appropriate times. Maggie, who knew everything about football, thought it was one of the most exciting games she had ever watched in her life. First the Ironmen scored on a field goal, but then the Wildcats came back with a touchdown and an extra point and took the lead. Then the Wildcats scored again, but the Ironmen caught the next kickoff and returned it for a touchdown. They followed that with an interception and a touchdown, but missed the extra point. The Wildcats crowd went wild.

"This is perfect," shouted Maggie as the game neared its end.

"What do you mean?" asked Lena frantically. "We're losing, aren't we? 14–16?"

"But there are only twenty seconds left in the game, and we have the ball at the fifteen yard line. All we have to do is kick a field goal to win. And our kicker is good enough to make it that far. Danville's using its last time-out. Come on. Let's jump down."

They had already positioned themselves near the bottom row of the bleachers, so it was easy to sneak between the benches and drop into the space underneath. Maggie pulled her headlamp out of her coat pocket, adjusted it on her head, and switched it on. She pointed the beam in the direction of the sprinkler fuse box. "We just—"

Maggie froze. Two unexpectedly large eyes glared back at her—the eyes of a dragon just before it eats its prey alive.

"Well," said a familiar voice. "Just the two I was expecting to see."

Maggie and Lena stared into the face of Mrs. Dornbusch. She stood before them in purple sweatpants, neon-green sneakers, an enormous, puffy purple parka, and a raspberry knitted hat with an oversize pom-pom sewn on the top. Suddenly another one of Mrs. Dornbusch's nicknames popped into Maggie's head: the Bleacher Beast.

"Lena and"—Mrs. Dornbusch squinted at the two girls—"not Mabel. Not Melissa. Not Morgan—" She waved her mittened hand, annoyed with their silly naming game. "This is where I watch all the home games, did you know that? Thirty-eight years of cheering on the Wildcats, but I don't like the crowds."

Maggie looked beyond Mrs. Dornbusch at the fuse box, bolted to one of the stanchions that held the bleachers in place. The Gray Gargoyle turned and looked at the fuse box, too. "I thought this was your work. Well designed, but poorly executed."

"Hey!" said Maggie, then slapped a gloved hand over her mouth to prevent any more damaging evidence from escaping.

"I think he's ready to kick!" shouted Lena, peering through the bleachers and legs of the spectators to the field beyond. "He's doing that warm-up kick thing."

Mrs. Dornbusch quickly turned to watch the final kick, and Maggie leaped past her to the fuse box, grabbing the electrical wire so that it would be at the ready. She wasn't about to let the crabby Dungeon Dragon ruin a perfectly good hack, not to mention the celebration of the year.

"And it's good!" the announcer crowed over the loudspeaker, as the bleachers began to reverberate with the Wildcat Beat. Odawahaka had won the game. Maggie plugged the wire into the outlet. Nothing could stop the hack now.

But then there was a whistle, and the voice over the PA announced, "Flag on the play." The crowd hushed. There were still three seconds left on the clock. The game wasn't over, and there was a penalty that could change everything.

The announcer relayed the official's call: "Unsportsmanlike conduct on the Wildcats. Fifteen-yard penalty. Replay the down."

A collective groan went up from the Wildcats side of the stands, while the Ironmen fans cheered and stamped their feet.

"What does that mean?" asked Lena.

Mrs. Dornbusch looked at Maggie and the fuse box. "It means you better pull the plug on whatever you have planned, because the kicker needs to make another field goal. And with an extra fifteen yards tacked on, he's out of his range. He'll never make a kick that long. And Odawahaka is going to lose its *only chance* of an undefeated season."

Maggie shook her head. "I can't unplug it. I mean, I can, but it won't do any good. The electrical wiring just jumps the starting motor. The hydraulic press runs on Freon, and—"

"Are you telling me—?"

"That an eight-foot rubber mouse is about to inflate

midfield, right where the kicker is lining up."

"This is bad, right?" asked Lena, looking from one to the other. "I don't know anything about football, but I can tell this is bad."

"What's the thrust?" demanded Mrs. Dornbusch.

"Two thousand pounds," admitted Maggie.

"Son of a monkey!" shouted Mrs. Dornbusch. "The ground is going to erupt right where that kicker is setting up, and he's going to get hurt." She pointed her mittened hand in the direction of the field. "And this town is going to lose its first undefeated season *ever.* *Maggie!*" She hurried out from under the bleachers to stop the game, and as she raced past, she said, "Just like your mother."

"Tell me what's happening on the field!" said Lena. "I can't stand to look."

Maggie peered between the bleachers. "The kicker is lined up!" she said frantically. "He's signaling that he's ready. Oh my gosh! Mrs. Dornbusch is rushing the field! She's screaming something, but no one can hear her. Oh no, the ground! It's starting to . . . bubble up. It's like it's breaking into bits! I don't think the players see it. The field goal kicker is going ahead anyway." Maggie gasped. "A security officer has Mrs. Dornbusch. Oh my gosh, she kicked him! He's limping, and I think he's swearing at her! But she got away! The football is sailing through the air . . ."

"And it's good!" shouted the PA announcer. For the second time in the last two minutes, the Wildcats crowd erupted in cheers. "That's a personal best for our Wildcats kicker and one that will go down in history for sure!"

Lena hugged Maggie, lifted her off the ground, and swung her around. Then the two girls lined up next to each other and performed the cheer that Maggie had taught Lena, complete with hand movements, turns, and a kick at the end: "Momentum equals mass times velocity! Go, Wildcats!"

The crowd was so overcome with joyful celebration—hugging, backslapping, and general noisemaking—that it failed to notice the growing gray blob in the middle of the field until it was nearly fully inflated. But Maggie and Lena watched, mesmerized.

"It's beautiful," whispered Lena, just as Mrs. Dornbusch reappeared under the bleachers, her raspberry knit cap missing, but otherwise unharmed.

"Well!" said Mrs. Dornbusch, breathing heavily. "At least I've still got a little *oomph* in this old body! But I'd say it's a pretty serious flaw in your design that you couldn't disable the mechanism once you started it," she added, wagging her mitten in Maggie's direction.

"I *can* disable the second part of the hack," said Maggie, "but at this point—"

There was an earthshaking gasp from the six thousand fans in the stands, and Maggie, Lena, and Mrs. Dornbusch looked to see that the sprinklers had turned on, spraying the entire football field and all the players from both teams.

"Let me guess," said Mrs. Dornbusch. "It isn't water coming out of those sprinklers."

Maggie shook her head, trying her best to keep a smile from curling her lips. She was edging toward the side of the stands. Lena was backing up in the opposite direction, not even trying to hide her smile. The Bleacher Beast couldn't catch them both—

"It's Moxie!" they shouted, then ran out onto the sidelines.

Maggie and Lena met on the field where the mouse had reached its full height of eight feet. Maggie could spot nearly every other sixth grader, along with their teachers and even Mrs. McDermott. Mr. Platt smiled and waved at her, giving her a big thumbs-up. Allie and Emily were standing with the high school chorus, which had broken out spontaneously in the traditional town anthem:

The river flows past us.
It flows to the sea.
From Odawahaka,
The land of the free.

Others in the stadium joined in the song, more and more of them, until the stadium rang out with the old-fashioned melody, learned for generations, that celebrated the small town and everything about it that made it dear to the people who lived there.

Many of the fans ventured onto the field. Those who liked Moxie leaned over the sprinklers as if they were giant water fountains and drank their fill, and those who didn't were happy to get soaked in the sticky stuff anyway.

"That's the thing about Moxie!" shouted Lena. "You either love it or you hate it!"

But Maggie had her eyes on the mouse. "It won't be long now," she whispered.

Lena grabbed Maggie's arm. "It's going to be spectacular."

"Unless it doesn't work," warned Maggie.

"It will work," said Lena simply. "I have faith." She squeezed Maggie's arm, and both girls held their breath.

The mouse inflated to 180 psi and then exploded in all its glory. Twenty-two pounds of glittery confetti (purple and silver, in honor of the Wildcats) sprayed out all over the field, sticking to the fans who were soaked in Moxie. A ROAR! rose up from the crowd.

Lena cheered, wildly dancing in circles around Maggie. "The perfect hack!"

Maggie was about to contradict Lena and repeat her father's firmly held belief that *no hack is perfect*, but she stopped herself. Watching the confetti sparkle as it floated through the air, listening to the song of joy and celebration sung by the entire stadium in unison, and seeing the simple happiness on the faces of the people she'd grown up with her whole life, she had to admit, yes, it was perfect.

"*Hack, perfectum!*" she shouted, then grabbed both of Lena's sticky hands and began swinging in circles, her long yellow hair flying out like party streamers caught up in the wind.

Maggie got home much later than she'd expected. It was well after eleven when she and Lena crept into the living room of Maggie's house and were surprised to find her mother asleep on the couch, an afghan pulled up to her chin.

"He-e-ey," said her mother, pushing herself to a sitting position while trying to wipe her hair out of her face and swipe away a tiny bit of drool that had dribbled across her cheek. "Look at you. What is all that stuff in your hair?"

"Confetti," said Maggie. "And anything else that will stick to high-fructose corn syrup. Which, it turns out, is pretty much everything on earth." She felt gross after the short bus ride home, but happy, too. The hack had been a huge success. "You missed the party."

"I know. I heard on the radio, though. It sounded like a blowout. Ha-ha!" She smiled at Lena. "I had something I had to work on."

"Hi, Mrs. Gallagher," said Lena. It seemed to Maggie that Lena and her mother exchanged a look before realizing that they should definitely *not* be looking at each other. Maggie stared at one, then the other.

"I'm going to my room," said Maggie. "And then I'm taking a shower. And then I'm going to bed. Forever."

"Okay!" said Lena, and she laughed in a very strange way, but didn't move to the door.

"I'll see you tomorrow?" asked Maggie.

"I think," said Lena, "that I'll just . . . get a Moxie for the road."

"You have *got* to be kidding," said Maggie as Lena

headed for the kitchen. Maggie turned to her mother. "I wish you'd been there. It was epic."

Her mother smiled. "Your dad used to say 'sublime,' when a hack went off perfectly. That's a Latin word. It means 'up to the very limit of perfection.' *Sublime*. What is it with engineers and Latin?"

Maggie knew. It was the language of people who built empires.

Her mother would never understand her the way her father would have, if he had lived. Engineers speak another language, she realized. *Hackito, ergo sum.* Her dad would have loved this night. Maggie was surprised when tears started to fill her eyes. "Good night, Mom," she said as she climbed the stairs. Lena would have to show herself out.

The hallway was dim and her tears made her vision blurry so that she missed her own doorway and came to the end of the hall where the bathroom was. She swung around. She wiped at her eyes. She reached out to turn on the hallway light.

There was no door.

In confusion, she looked down to the other end of the hallway. There was the door to her mother's bedroom. There was the hallway closet. Behind her, the bathroom door stood slightly ajar. Everything was exactly the way it had always been in this house. Except that the door to her bedroom had disappeared.

Like a blind person reaching out into unfamiliar territory, she spread both hands and touched the wall where the door should have been. The wallpaper felt smooth under her fingers as it always did. There was the sleepy Little Boy Blue. There were the sheep in the meadow, and there, the cows in the corn.

She heard a giggle. She turned. Lena and her mother were peering up at her from the landing on the stairs. Lena's smile was so wide it looked like she could swallow a minivan. Her mother was smiling, too, but more carefully, as if she had something to lose.

"You . . . you . . . hacked my door?" asked Maggie slowly.

"It was your mother's idea!" shouted Lena, unable to hold back her glee. "She asked for my help, but I hardly did anything, just printed up the wallpaper. She's been working on it all week."

Maggie ran her fingers carefully over the surface of the paper, reaching wider and wider from the center of where she knew her door was supposed to be. She couldn't feel a single seam. The pattern matched up perfectly. It was completely undetectable. *Sublime.*

"I sanded down all the edges," said her mother.

"Then I used this special matte varnish adhesive that causes the roughed-up fibers to sort of meld together."

"It must have taken you hours," said Maggie.

Her mother nodded, looking closely at Maggie's face, waiting.

"You did this for me?" asked Maggie.

"You're my daughter. I'd do anything for you."

Maggie didn't know what to say or do. She had never had this feeling before, the feeling that her mother actually understood her. It was bewildering. "Oh, Mom," she said awkwardly. Then she rushed down the half flight of stairs and hugged her mother hard, neither one minding the horrible stickiness of the gooey Moxie that coated them both.

"I'm going to cry!" shouted Lena. "Seriously. The tears are about to start gushing out of my eyes!"

"You like it?" asked her mother, squeezing Maggie.

"It's perfect," said Maggie. "I didn't know you were a hacker."

"Oh, honey," said her mother, stroking Maggie's hair. "There's lots and lots of stuff you don't know about me."

Later that night, after showering, Maggie was lying on the sofa in the living room. She had decided to sleep downstairs because she couldn't bear to undo her mother's hack yet. It was too fantastic, and she wanted to examine it in the light of day.

Maggie had just entered that am-I-asleep-or-am-I-awake phase, when her cell phone rang. It was Lena.

"Maggie?" she asked. "Did you hear they made the B-1 Bomber the principal of Oda M?"

"No!" said Maggie, trying to keep her voice low because her mother had gone to bed. *Oh, are we in trouble.*

"I bet she's the only one who would take the job," said Lena. Maggie heard the bounce of bedsprings and imagined Lena in her rainbow world, surrounded by all the colors of the prism.

"That's because she's the only one who isn't afraid of mice!" Maggie rolled over on the couch, burrowing under the blankets her mother had tucked in for her.

"She isn't afraid of anything!" said Lena, and they laughed, retelling the story of how the Dungeon Dragon had tackled the security officer.

Both girls grew quiet for a moment, in that way that happens late at night.

"Maggie?"

"Yeah."

"I miss the Mouse."

"Me too." What would come next, now that the Mouse was no more? During the celebration on the football field, the sixth graders had agreed to abolish the office of class president and have a student council instead. That way, everyone could have a voice in making the school a better place. Even Kayla had agreed to the change. After all, she didn't want to be class president just because the real winner exploded.

There was something else on Maggie's mind, too, but she wasn't sure how to bring it up. Finally, she decided just to ask. "Lena? When Principal Shute said that stuff about your family—that there were 'oddities'—what was he talking about?"

Maggie could hear Lena take a deep breath in. "The next time we're together, I'll tell you all about it. But not tonight. Okay?"

"Okay," said Maggie. "Tonight, we celebrate!"

"Hackito, ergo sum gaudium!"

"What *is* it with artists and Latin?" asked Maggie, laughing. She paused for a minute. "I'm really glad you moved to town. You know why? Because you are nothing but trouble, Lena Polachev."

And I wouldn't have it any other way.

ACKNOWLEDGMENTS

I want to begin by thanking the entire town of Berwick, Pennsylvania, and most particularly Dr. Holly Morrison, previously the principal at Fourteenth Street Elementary School, and Dara Scala, the Title 1 Reading Specialist at Fourteenth Street, who invited me to their district in 2014 to visit Berwick's four elementary schools. This was my first experience of the necklace of small towns in central Pennsylvania that follow the Susquehanna River as it winds its way from its headwaters in Upstate New York to its final destination, the Chesapeake Bay in Maryland. Most of the Susquehanna's 464 miles flow through Pennsylvania, and if it sounds as though I'm thanking a river in these acknowledgments, I suppose I am. But more specifically, I'm thanking the many people—too many to name—who live along its route and who talked to me with great openness and generosity about what it's like to live in a small town that has fallen on hard times.

Many will notice that the fictional town of Odawahaka bears more than a passing resemblance to Catawissa, Pennsylvania. That's because Allison Burrell, librarian and media specialist at Southern Columbia Middle School in Catawissa, was brave enough to answer a desperate, last-minute request from an author she'd never met: *Could I please spend a day at your middle school, attending classes, and perhaps even meeting with some of your students? I'm writing this book, you see . . .* She kindly—and with great speed—secured approval, made the arrangements, and smoothed my path in every way, and for this, I am eternally grateful. A very special thanks to Madison Colella, Allyson Kranzel, Stephanie Dunkelberger, Lear Quinton, Ty Roadarmel, Max Tillett, Amelia Esposito, and Kayla Gallagher, who all gave up a precious lunch period to talk to the peculiar author who wondered what it was like to be thirteen years old in a small town in central Pennsylvania. These students were friendly, funny, open, generous, and spirited. I hope I was able to capture their love of their hometowns on the page. I myself fell in love with the town and borrowed liberally the names of its streets, its businesses,

294

its geography, and its points of interest. So, thank you, Catawissa.

Odawahaka Middle School, I want to be clear, is completely *unlike* the beautiful middle school that students in Catawissa attend. Oda M, rather, is a gothic fantasy that reflects some of the reality of small towns across the country, but more so the dark passage of time and the sad truth of what happens when we fail to adapt and change and grow with present-day circumstances.

I'd like to thank Ariane Oliver, Latin teacher at Wellesley High School, Peter Caccavale, Latin teacher at Needham High School, and Matthew Webb, Latin instructor for the public schools of Brookline. All three helped me with the Latin translations in the book. Any mistakes that appear in the text are entirely my own. *Mea culpa.* (I did that one all by myself.) And thank you to Deborah Douglas, director of collections and curator of science and technology at the MIT Museum, who answered my questions and provided invaluable sources for information about famous hacks at the Massachusetts Institute of Technology. To all who are interested in achieving the unachievable, I highly recommend the book *Nightwork: A History of Hacks and Pranks at MIT*, by T. F. Peterson and published by the MIT Press.

Thank you to the members of my writers group

who read the first draft of this book and helped, as they always do, to make it better: Sarah Lamstein, Tracey Fern, and Carol Peacock.

And a giant—and ongoing—thank-you to my editor, Maria Barbo, and her assistant, Rebecca Schwarz, at HarperCollins. When Maria and I first discussed the idea of writing a book about two middle school girls who can't help but get into trouble, I said I wanted to set the story in a small town in central Pennsylvania, the kind of place where all that is wonderful about small-town America exists alongside the struggles and despair of such places. She was fully on board from the beginning, and her support never waivered. For that, I say, *Thank you, Maria.*

ACTIVITIES

#1: WHY MAGGIE LOVES SIR ISAAC NEWTON

Sir Isaac Newton (1643–1727) was an English physicist and mathematician. He was smart, observant, and had *great* hair.

One of the things he liked to observe was what happens to an object (like a ball) when different **forces** (like gravity, friction, tension, or magnetism) act on it. Some of these observations became important **laws of physics** that help explain why things do the things they do.

Maggie and Sir Isaac both love laws and equations. They're very useful when planning a hack!

Newton's First Law of Motion says that an object at rest will stay at rest and an object in motion will stay in motion as long as all the forces acting on it are *balanced*. But what about when they're not?

That's why Maggie loves **Newton's Second Law of Motion:** Acceleration (think of it as a change in speed) occurs when *unbalanced* forces act on an object.

$$(FORCE) = (MASS) \times (ACCELERATION)$$

Maggie has a hack in mind. She wants to catapult a rubber mouse through Mrs. Dornbusch's open window and have it land on her desk with great force.

She has two mice and two catapults. The first mouse weighs 5 ounces and the first catapult can accelerate any mouse at a rate of 10 meters/second/second. The second mouse weighs 10 ounces and the second catapult can accelerate any mouse at a rate of 5 m/s/s.

Which mouse will land on Mrs. Dornbusch's desk with the greatest force?

Hey, here's a follow-up question: Can you think of a better plan for Maggie's hack? And what will you title the picture that Lena takes of Mrs. Dornbusch's reaction?

*Answer: Both mice will land with exactly the same force. The better plan is to use the **heavier** mouse with the **faster** catapult. That will create the greatest force—and get the funniest reaction out of Mrs. Dornbusch.*

#2: WHAT IF MIDDLE SCHOOL OBSERVED THE LAWS OF MOTION?

Maggie loves Newton's Second Law of Motion:

$$(FORCE) = (MASS) \times (ACCELERATION)$$

Just for fun, try to imagine that this law applies to problems at Oda M!

Think of each of the following problems as a ball (that's the object with a certain size or *mass*), each of the following people as a *force*, and the results as change in direction (that's what we'll call *acceleration*).

Some of the problems are BIG and will need a lot of *force* to create a change. Some of the problems are SMALL and won't require much to move the ball.

Some of the forces are STRONG and others are WEAK. (Think about how much force you exert when you really care versus when you don't.)

So consider each of the following situations. How BIG is the problem? How STRONG are the forces acting in opposite directions?

Now make your best guess: In which direction do you think the ball will roll? There are no right or wrong answers, so have fun and discuss with your friends!

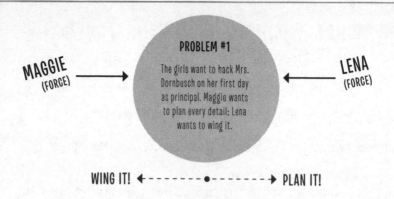

PROBLEM #1

The girls want to hack Mrs. Dornbusch on her first day as principal. Maggie wants to plan every detail; Lena wants to wing it.

MAGGIE (FORCE)

LENA (FORCE)

WING IT! ←- - - - - - - ● - - - - - - → PLAN IT!

Will spontaneous and artistic Lena convince Maggie to wing it? Or will Maggie win over Lena with logic and reason?

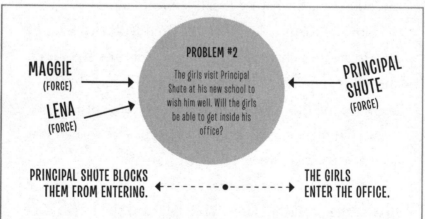

PROBLEM #2

The girls visit Principal Shute at his new school to wish him well. Will the girls be able to get inside his office?

MAGGIE (FORCE)

LENA (FORCE)

PRINCIPAL SHUTE (FORCE)

PRINCIPAL SHUTE BLOCKS THEM FROM ENTERING. ←- - - - - - ● - - - - - → THE GIRLS ENTER THE OFFICE.

How much do you think Maggie and Lena care about wishing Mr. Shute well? How much do you think he *never wants to see either of them again*?

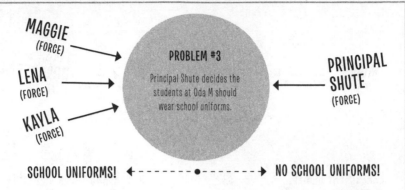

SCHOOL UNIFORMS! ←-------●-------→ NO SCHOOL UNIFORMS!

Do you think Kayla wants to give up her fabulous wardrobe? What if Maggie had to dress like everyone else? What if Lena could never wear her *Dada Is My Daddy* T-shirt? Who do you think will win this fight?

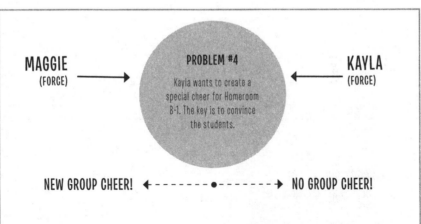

NEW GROUP CHEER! ←-------●-------→ NO GROUP CHEER!

Will there be a new group cheer or not? Who is more passionate about this problem, Maggie or Kayla? How hard will it be to convince the students in B-1?

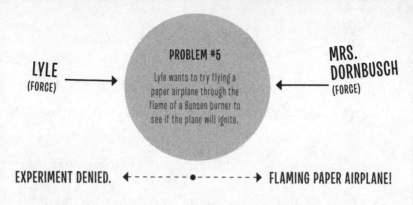

LYLE
(FORCE)

PROBLEM #5

Lyle wants to try flying a
paper airplane through the
flame of a Bunsen burner to
see if the plane will ignite.

MRS.
DORNBUSCH
(FORCE)

EXPERIMENT DENIED. ◄ - - - - - - ● - - - - - - ► FLAMING PAPER AIRPLANE!

This one is tough! Will Lyle succeed in lighting
a paper airplane on fire? Will Mrs. Dornbusch care
enough to stop him? You be the judge!

#3: HOW TO MAKE A DADA POEM

Dada was an art movement that began during World War I and continued into the early 1920s. It was an explosive reaction to the horrors of the war and embraced freedom by deliberately breaking rules and creating purposeful silliness. Unlike Maggie, followers of Dada believed that random chance could lead to excellent outcomes.

With this idea in mind, poets such as Tristan Tzara arranged words randomly to create Dada poems. Some people considered these poems to be nonsense while others believed they freed us from the idea that poetry (or anything) had to be the way it always had been. What do you think?

If you like, try creating a Dada poem yourself. Here's an updated version of Tzara's original instructions:

- Find a newspaper, book, old journal entry, or article printed from the internet.
- Take a pair of scissors.
- Choose a paragraph (or section) that is as long as you want your poem to be.
- Cut out the paragraph.
- Cut out each individual word in the paragraph.

- Put the pieces in a bag.
- Shake gently.
- Next pull out the pieces, one by one.
- Carefully write down the words in the exact order you took them from the bag. No cheating!
- *Ta-da!* Dada! You are now the author of an infinitely original poem.

What do you think? Is it nonsense or does it express something about you or the world?

Here is a Dada poem created from a recent newspaper article:

> *listening*
> *plunging*
> *download while the few been*
> *streaming recorded theme*
>
> *online habits*
> *business the CD*
>
> *and*
>
> *shot the last sales*
>
> *has in up*
> *has for that shift years*
> *were quickly prevailing as music*

#4: ARE YOU A SECRET DADAIST?

Take this quick quiz to find out if you have what it takes to hang with Lena and challenge the status quo!

1. When you were little and played with blocks, your favorite thing to do was:
   - A. build towers with the blocks
   - B. knock the block towers down
   - C. build the towers and then knock them down
   - D. I refuse to acknowledge the existence of blocks.

2. In your opinion, which of the following is an example of great poetry?
   - A. Shall I compare thee to a summer's day?
   - B. O Captain! my Captain! our fearful trip is done
   - C. Once upon a midnight dreary, while I pondered, weak and weary,
   - D. penguin narrow and standoff rattling boots justice flawed is his said no tweets destroy!

3. Which gift would you most like to receive?

    A. a really good book

    B. a new bike

    C. a gift certificate to your favorite clothing store

    D. a toilet seat to hang on the wall

4. If you could have tickets to any concert, which concert would you choose?

    A. The Foo Fighters

    B. Adele

    C. One Direction

    D. fifty-two people who are not musicians playing random notes on different instruments at exactly the same time

5. If you could choose to eat any dessert, you would choose:

    A. chocolate ice cream

    B. apple pie

    C. vanilla cake with strawberry frosting

    D. raisins, olives, and potato chips covered in ketchup and maple syrup and topped with a postage stamp

6. In your opinion, the greatest threat the world faces is:

    A. the invasion of Martians

    B. a zombie apocalypse

    C. a mutant virus

    D. war

7. Which of these statements is true?

    A. The month after July is August.

    B. A triangle has three sides.

    C. If $a = b$, then $b = a$.

    D. There is no such thing as truth.

8. If a person in authority tells you to do something, you will:

    A. do it

    B. ask the person "why?"

    C. decide for yourself whether it is the right thing to do

    D. run in circles like a chicken with its head cut off screaming at the top of your lungs: "funhouse messy lightning old shoes!"

9. If faced with the problem of being lost in the wilderness, you would:

> A. stay in one place in the hopes of being found
>
> B. hike in the hopes that you would find your way back to civilization
>
> C. choose to live the rest of your life in the wilderness
>
> D. write a manifesto about why a primitive life is superior to all others

10. If you were walking down the street and found an empty bottle of Moxie that someone had tossed on the side of the road, you would say:

> A. "People shouldn't litter!"
>
> B. "Boy, I wish I had a Moxie to drink!"
>
> C. "I can reuse that bottle as a vase for some flowers."
>
> D. "Hey, look! It's art!"

Count the number of times you answered D. Check your score below:

> 0–1: You are not a Dadaist. You like order and rational thought. Good for you!
>
> 2–4: Mostly, you like to follow the straight and

narrow, but every once in a while you take a walk on the Dada side.

5–7: Yep, you are definitely in training to become a Dadaist.

8–10: Proceed directly to the last house on 2½ Street. Lena is waiting for you, because you are definitely a Dadaist and *nothing but trouble*!

Curious about the poems quoted in question 2?

A. William Shakespeare, Sonnet 18

B. Walt Whitman, "O Captain! My Captain!"

C. Edgar Allan Poe, "The Raven"

D. Jacqueline Davies, untitled

"Well-behaved women seldom make history."
—Laurel Thatcher Ulrich, historian, 1976

Maggie would definitely agree with those words. Who wants to behave when getting into trouble leads to all kinds of history-making results? Here's a list of a few Margarets who reached for the stars and broke all sorts of barriers!

MARGARET BROWN (1867-1932), PHILANTHROPIST, ACTIVIST

"The Unsinkable Molly Brown," as she became known, survived the 1912 *Titanic* disaster, earning a reputation for bravery and strength as she helped evacuate many passengers before climbing into a lifeboat herself. Later in her life, she continued to be a force of nature, educating children, promoting workers' and women's rights, and rebuilding areas in France devastated by World War I.

MARGARET MEAD (1901-1978), ANTHROPOLOGIST

In 1925, Margaret Mead blazed a path for female anthropologists by setting off to do fieldwork in Samoa. During her long career, she studied the cultures of many different people all over the world. She became an influential speaker and writer in the 1960s and 1970s. The following quotation is widely attributed to her: "Never doubt that a small group of thoughtful, committed citizens can change the world; indeed, it's the only thing that ever has." The Mouse would certainly agree with that.

MARGARET HAMILTON (1902-1985), ACTRESS

Schoolteacher turned witch? Yep, that's just what this Margaret did. After working as a kindergarten teacher, Hamilton turned to acting, eventually landing the role of the Wicked Witch of the West in the classic film *The Wizard of Oz*. The American Film Institute named the Wicked Witch the greatest female movie villain of all time. Despite her villainous side, Hamilton remained committed to education throughout her life and served as both a school board member and a Sunday school teacher.

MARGARET BOURKE-WHITE (1904-1971), PHOTOGRAPHER

This Margaret liked to be *first*. She was the first foreigner allowed to enter the Soviet Union to photograph its industry. She was the first American woman to be a war photojournalist. And she was the first woman to have her photographs appear in *Life* magazine. In fact, she provided the cover photo for the magazine's debut issue in November 1936. As a photographer, Margaret was fearless in her attempts to get the best shot: She would climb to terrifying heights, squeeze herself into tight spaces, creep out on precarious riggings, and travel all over the world. Her photos were artistic, powerful, and one of a kind.

MARGARET WISE BROWN (1910-1952), CHILDREN'S AUTHOR

Known by the nickname "Brownie," Margaret Wise Brown published over one hundred children's books, including *Goodnight Moon* and *The Runaway Bunny*. Deceptively simple and seemingly offhand, her text had a way of speaking directly to children in language they understood. Never preachy, often funny and offbeat, many of her books remain classics more than half a century after they were first published.

MARGARET WALKER (1915-1998), POET

Margaret Walker's first published book of poetry, *For My People*, blew everyone's socks off. She was just twenty-seven when the book won the Yale Series of Younger Poets Award, making her the first black woman in American literary history to win a prestigious national competition. For thirty years she taught literature, and toward the end of her career, she wrote *Jubilee*, which the *Washington Post* called "the first truly historical black American novel."

MARGARET THATCHER (1925-2013), PRIME MINISTER OF GREAT BRITAIN

Born the daughter of a grocer in England in 1925, Margaret Thatcher rose through the ranks of British politics to become the longest-serving British prime minister of the twentieth century and the first woman ever to hold that office. She was both wildly popular and equally unpopular during her tenure, but through it all, she was a tough leader and a strong negotiator, earning her the nickname "the Iron Lady."

MARGARET COURT (B. 1942), TENNIS CHAMPION

Ranked number one in the world by the Women's Tennis Association for seven years, Margaret Court dominated tennis in the 1960s and 1970s. She was the first woman since the open era to win a singles Grand Slam (which is all four major tournaments in the same year). In fact, over her long career, she won twenty-four major singles tournaments titles, a record that still stands.

MARGARET RHEA SEDDON (B. 1947), PHYSICIAN, ASTRONAUT

Margaret Rhea Seddon was one of the first six women who entered the NASA astronaut program in 1978. She flew on the space shuttle three times, as both a mission specialist and a payload commander. Seddon, now retired from NASA, spent a total of thirty days, two hours, and twenty-one minutes in space. Very cool.

MARGARET CHO (B. 1968), COMEDIAN

Stand-up comedy is definitely a place for breaking rules, and Margaret Cho does just that—while making people laugh. Born in San Francisco into a Korean family, Cho was bullied as a child. "I was hurt because I was different, and so sharing my experience . . . heals others when they hear it—those who are suffering right now." Her comedy focuses on social and political issues, in particular race, and she has won many awards for her work on behalf of women, Asians, and the LGBT community.